THE ADVENTURES OF
JONNIE ROCKET

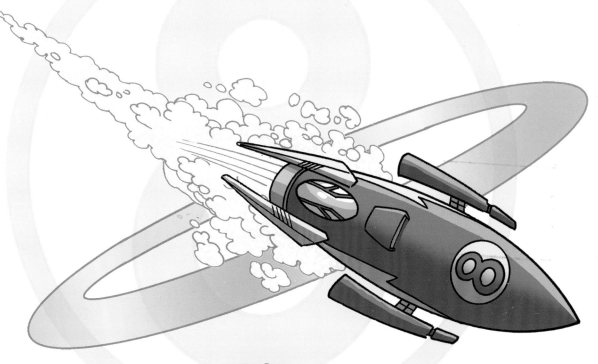

THE
SEA OF SARGOSS

The Sea of Sargoss

Character copyright © 2000 John Chapman

Artwork copyright © 2013 John Chapman

Text copyright © 2013 John Chapman

Author and creator John Chapman

Illustrations by The Comic Stripper Studio

A CIP catalogue record of this book is available from the British Library

ISBN: 978-0-9573035-3-9

Published by Jonnie Rocket Ltd. 2013

Printed by DCW Penrose & Co. Ltd. Staines, Middlesex

First edition: 2013

www.jonnierocket.com

Meet the Cast!

Jonnie
Rocket

Dr Avatar

Queen of
Sargoss

Slick
Scarlet

Bosun
Bone Head

Gunner
Galumph

Skeletor
Man

Tyrant
Tash

Egrod
the Eel

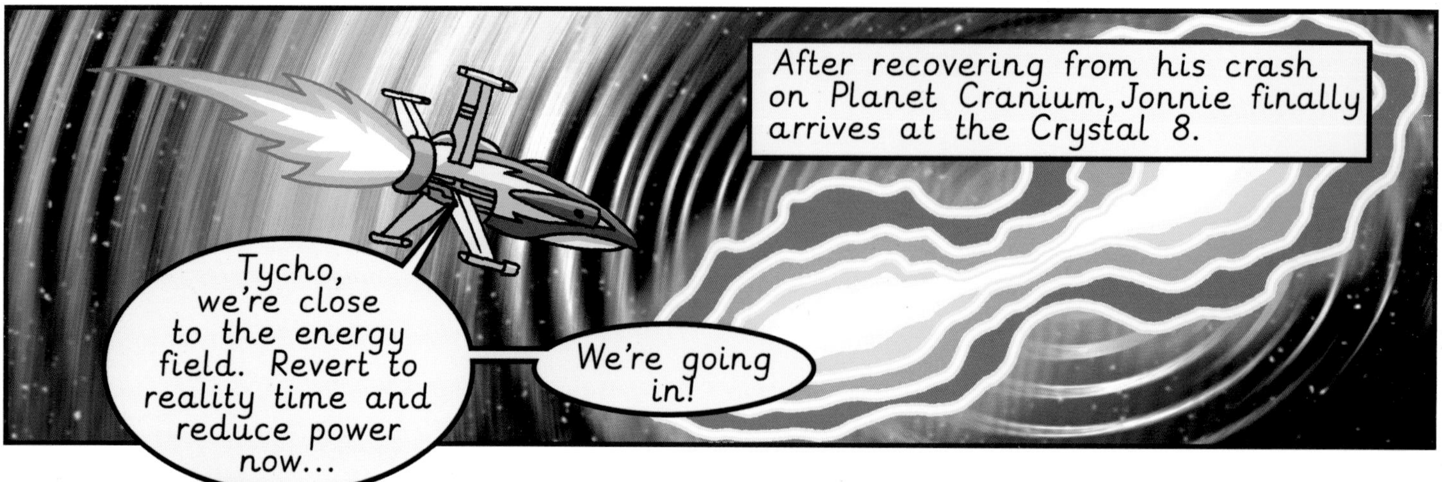
After recovering from his crash on Planet Cranium, Jonnie finally arrives at the Crystal 8.
Tycho, we're close to the energy field. Revert to reality time and reduce power now...
We're going in!

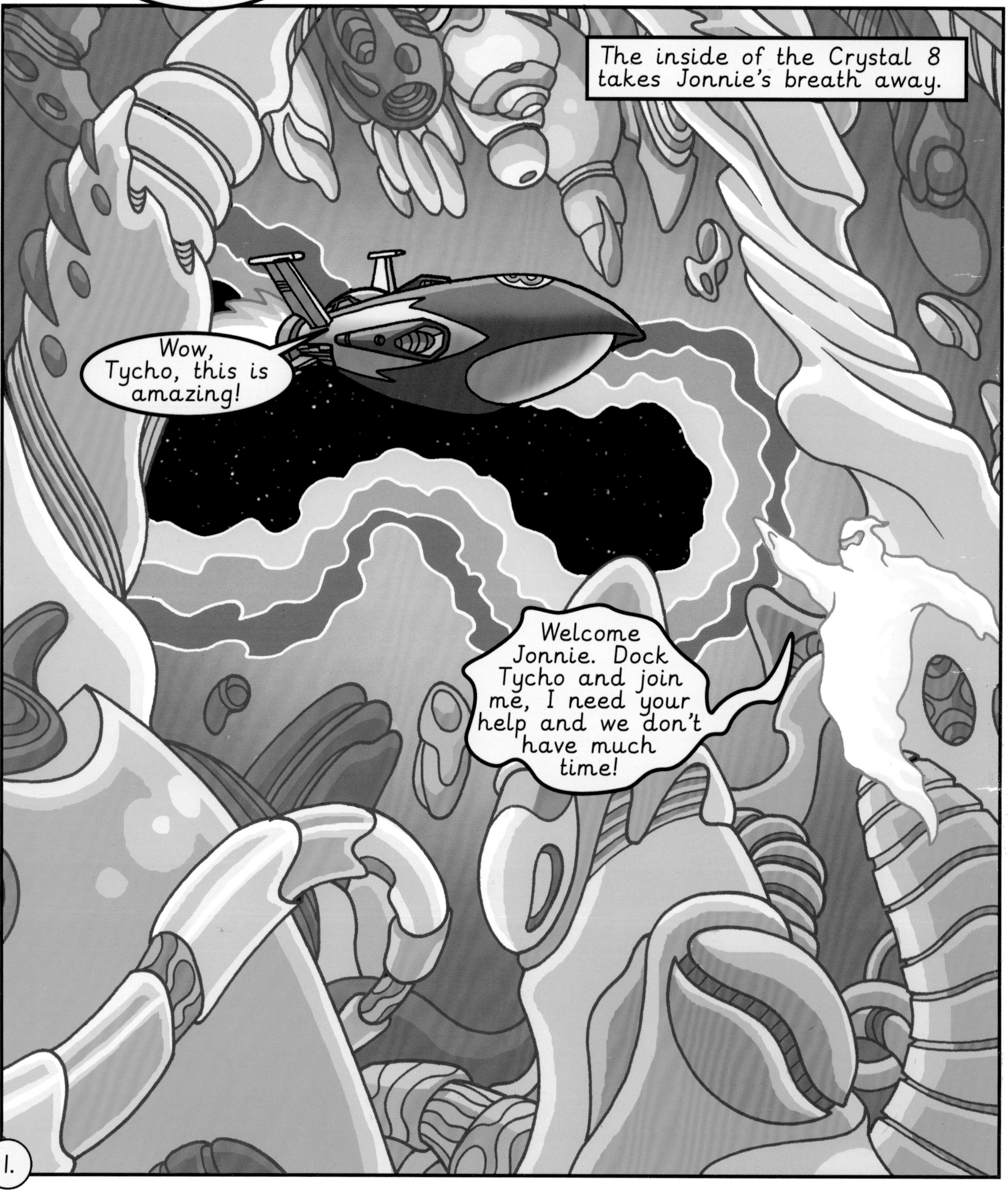
The inside of the Crystal 8 takes Jonnie's breath away.
Wow, Tycho, this is amazing!
Welcome Jonnie. Dock Tycho and join me, I need your help and we don't have much time!

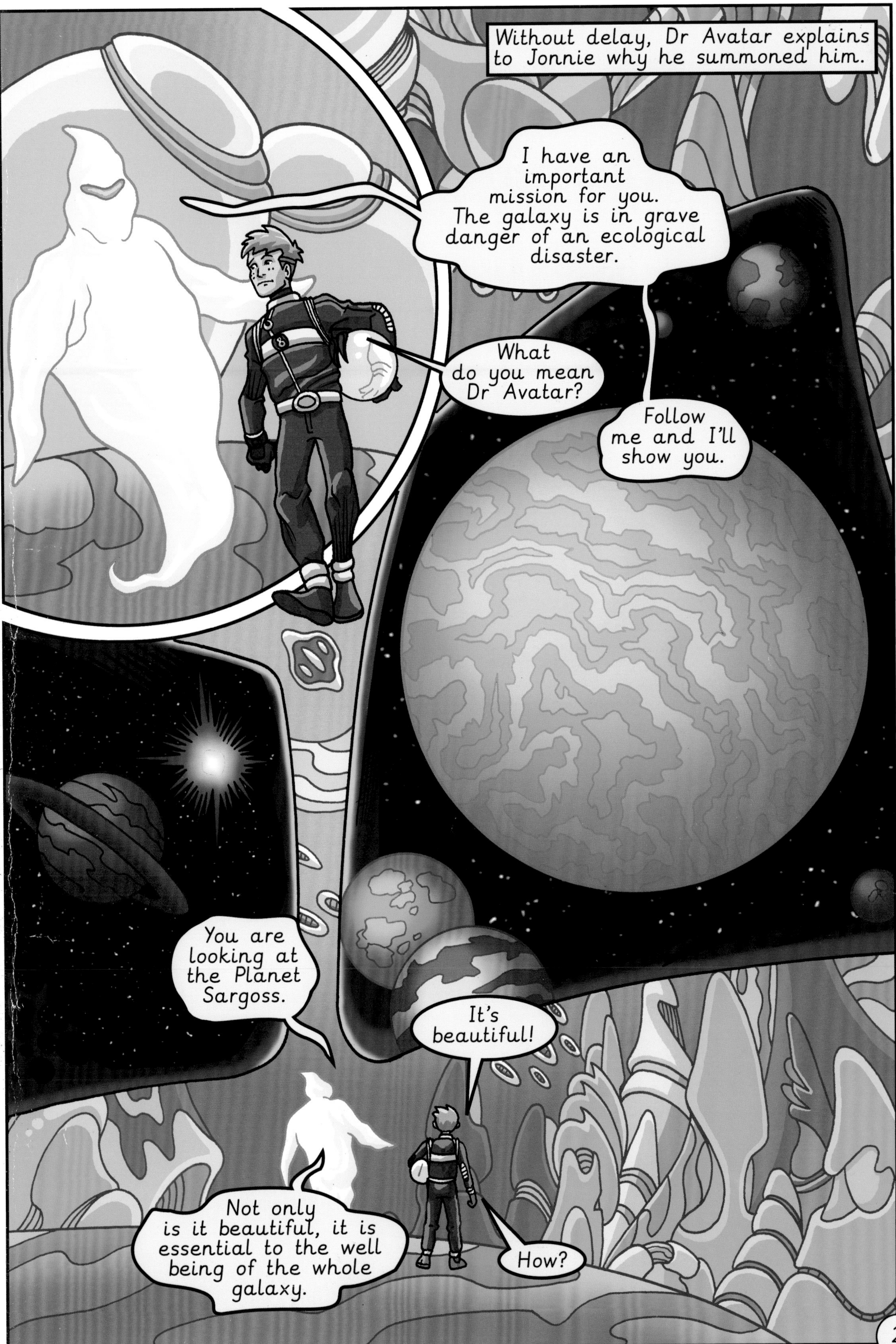
Without delay, Dr Avatar explains to Jonnie why he summoned him.
I have an important mission for you. The galaxy is in grave danger of an ecological disaster.
What do you mean Dr Avatar?
Follow me and I'll show you.
You are looking at the Planet Sargoss.
It's beautiful!
Not only is it beautiful, it is essential to the well being of the whole galaxy.
How?

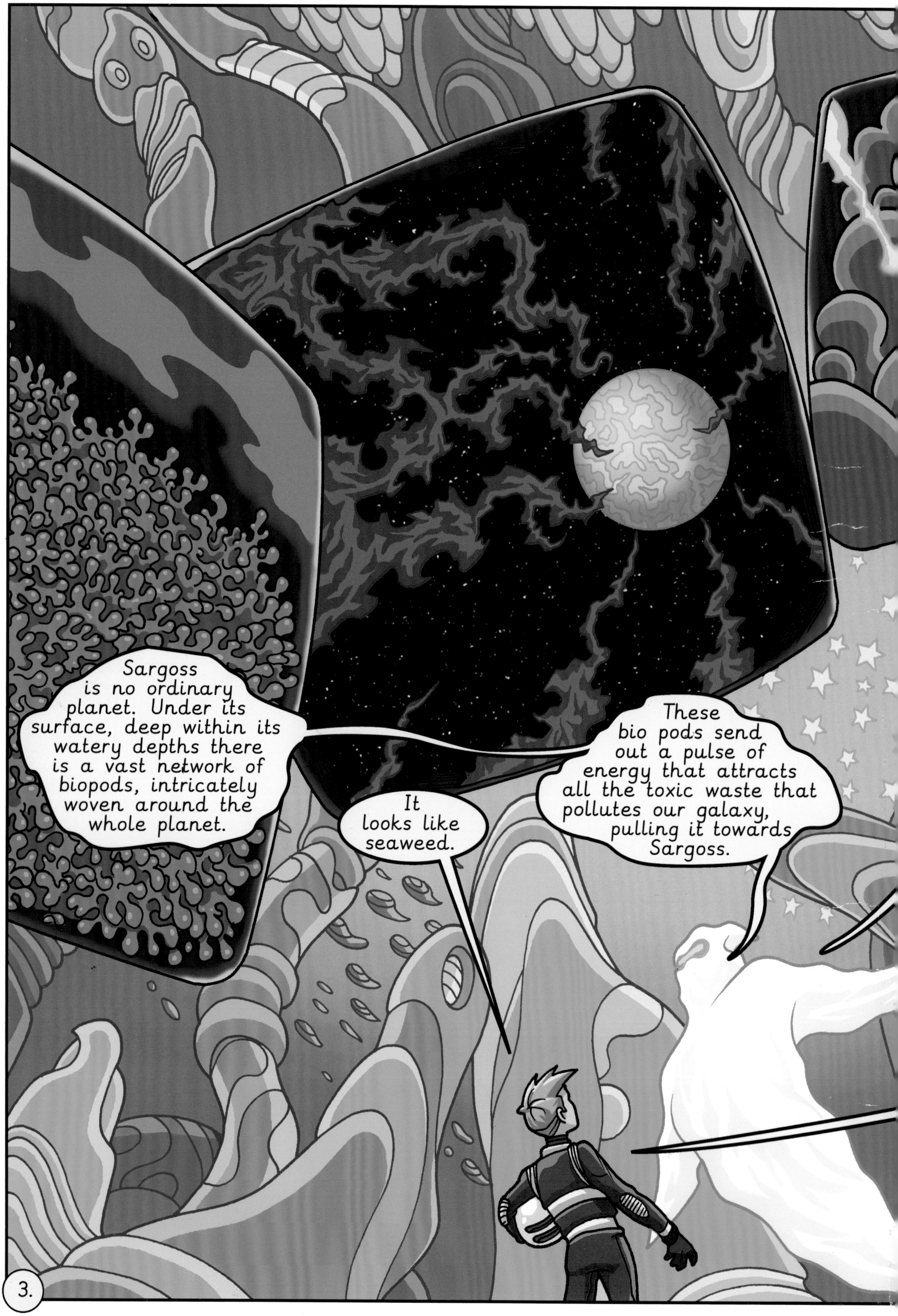
Sargoss is no ordinary planet. Under its surface, deep within its watery depths there is a vast network of biopods, intricately woven around the whole planet.
It looks like seaweed.
These bio pods send out a pulse of energy that attracts all the toxic waste that pollutes our galaxy, pulling it towards Sargoss.

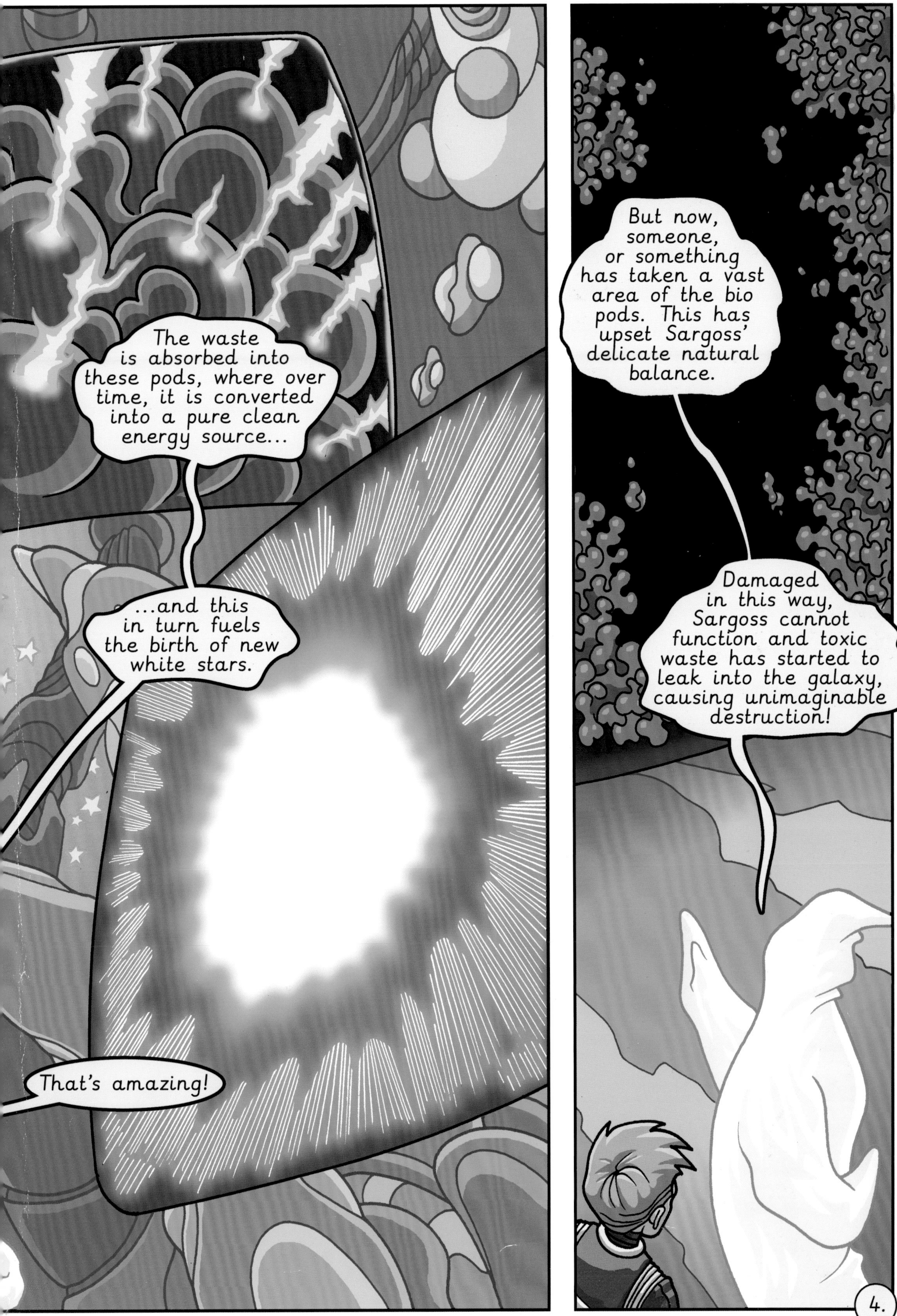
The waste is absorbed into these pods, where over time, it is converted into a pure clean energy source...
...and this in turn fuels the birth of new white stars.
That's amazing!
But now, someone, or something has taken a vast area of the bio pods. This has upset Sargoss' delicate natural balance.
Damaged in this way, Sargoss cannot function and toxic waste has started to leak into the galaxy, causing unimaginable destruction!

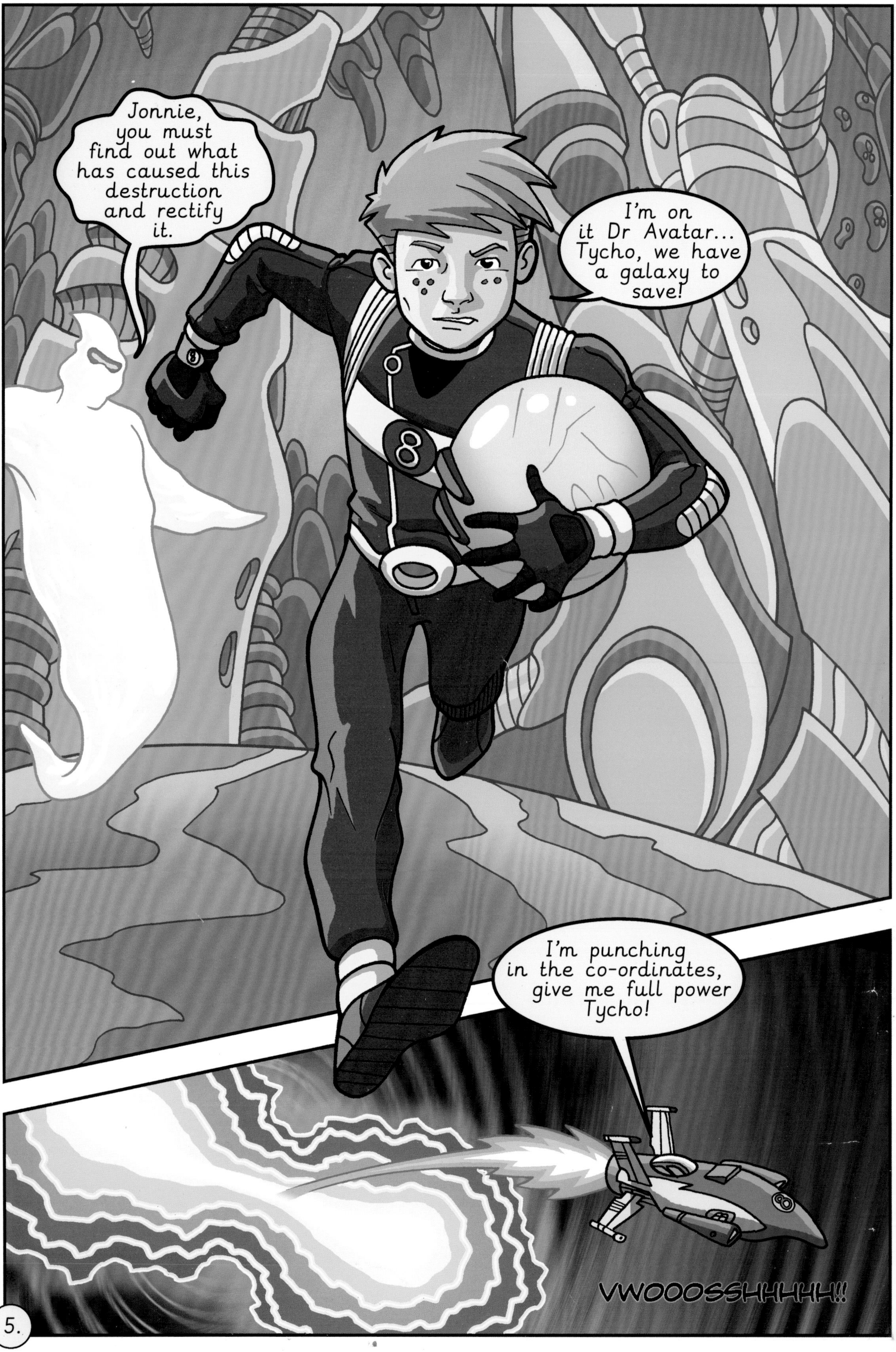
Jonnie, you must find out what has caused this destruction and rectify it.
I'm on it Dr Avatar... Tycho, we have a galaxy to save!
I'm punching in the co-ordinates, give me full power Tycho!
VWOOOSSHHHHH!!

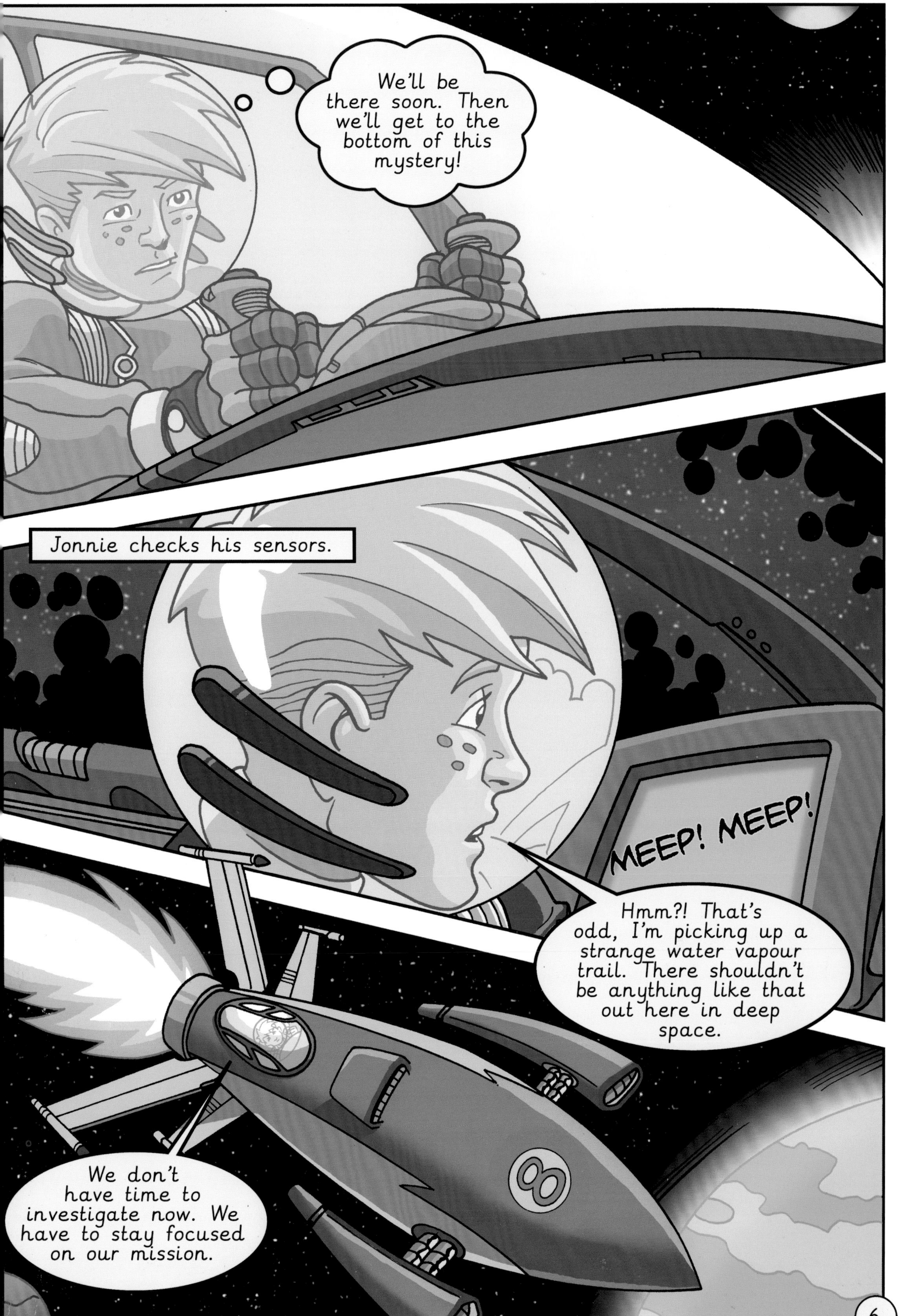

We'll be there soon. Then we'll get to the bottom of this mystery!
Jonnie checks his sensors.
MEEP! MEEP!
Hmm?! That's odd, I'm picking up a strange water vapour trail. There shouldn't be anything like that out here in deep space.
We don't have time to investigate now. We have to stay focused on our mission.
8

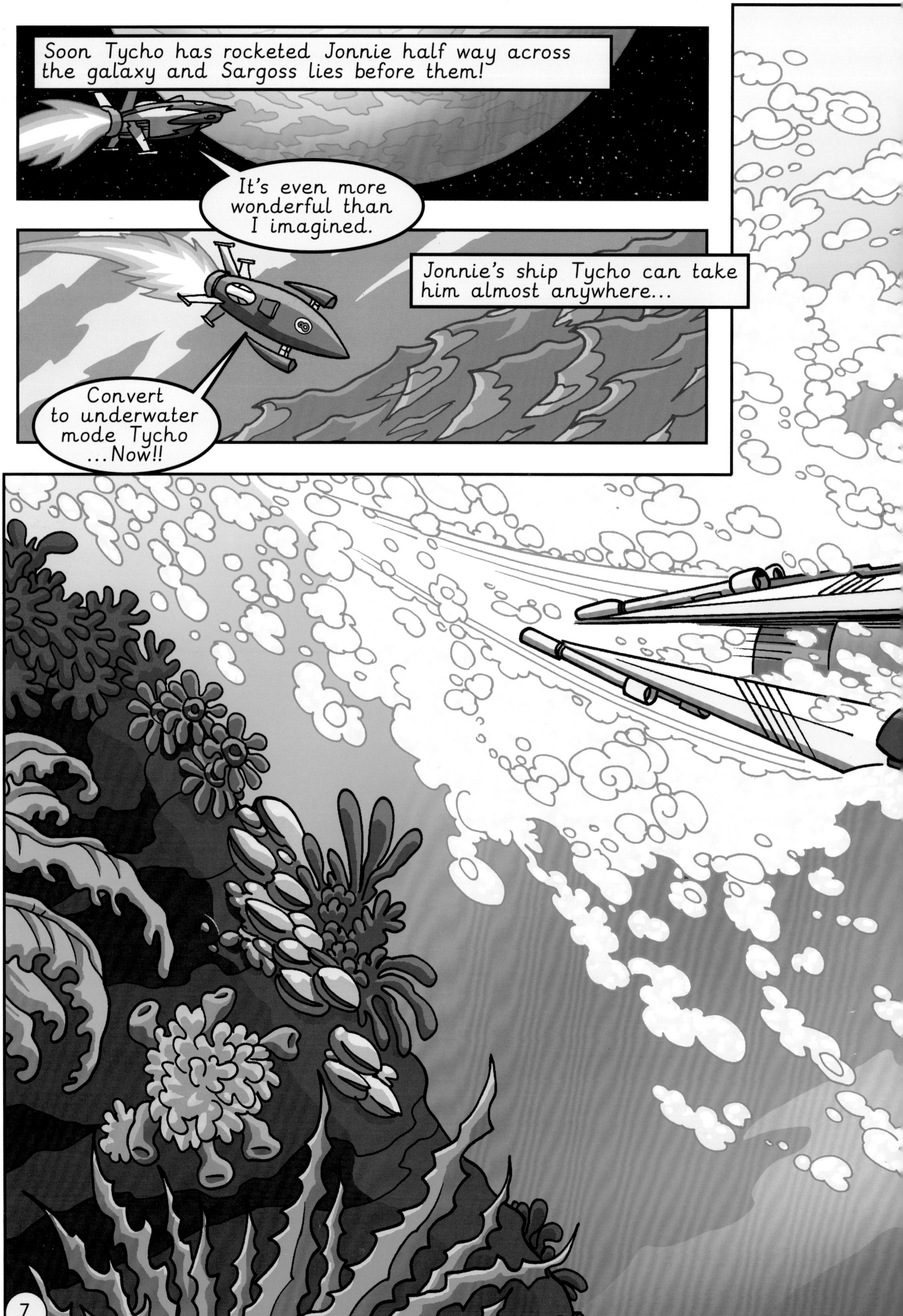
Soon Tycho has rocketed Jonnie half way across the galaxy and Sargoss lies before them!
It's even more wonderful than I imagined.
Jonnie's ship Tycho can take him almost anywhere...
Convert to underwater mode Tycho ...Now!!

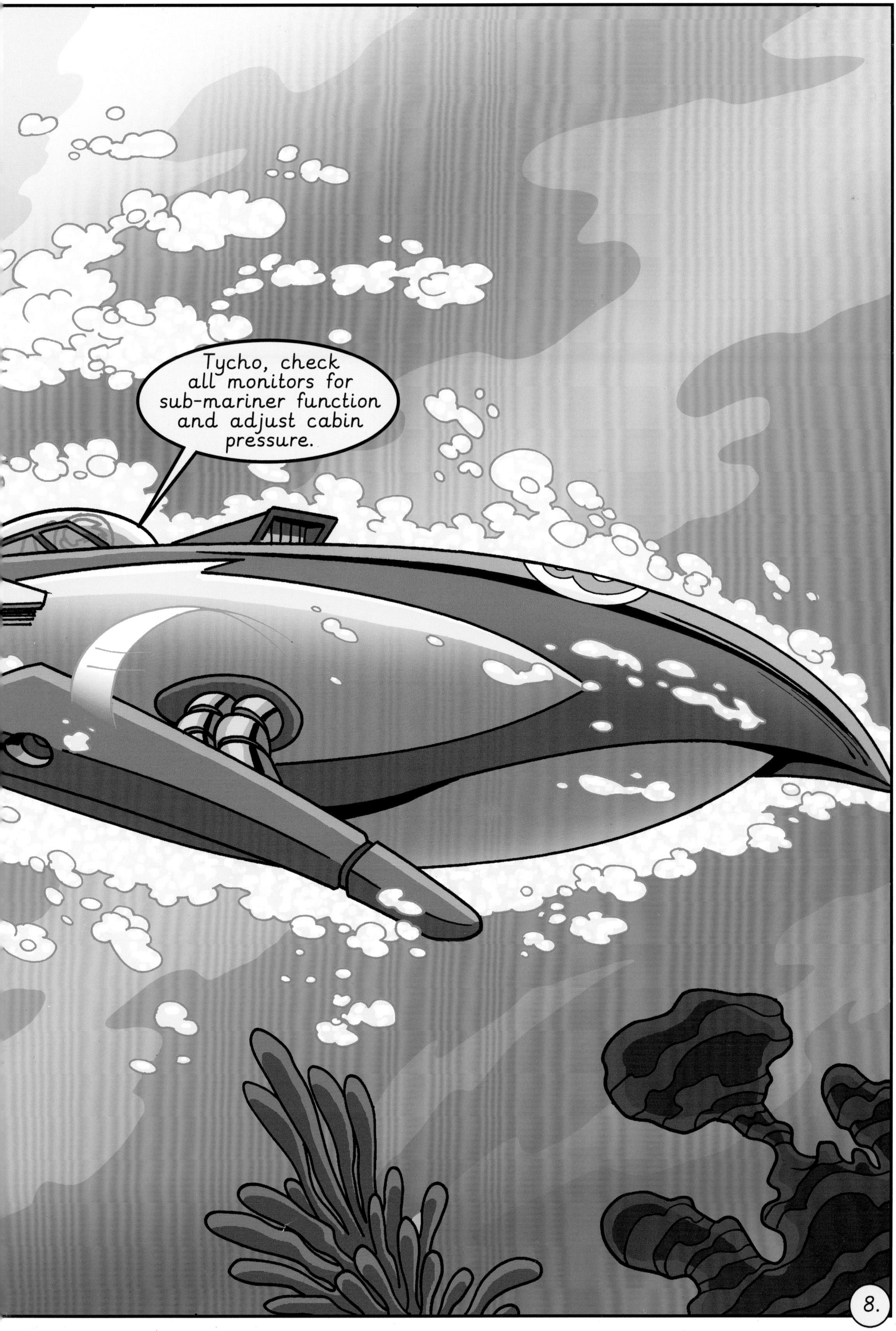
Tycho, check all monitors for sub-mariner function and adjust cabin pressure.

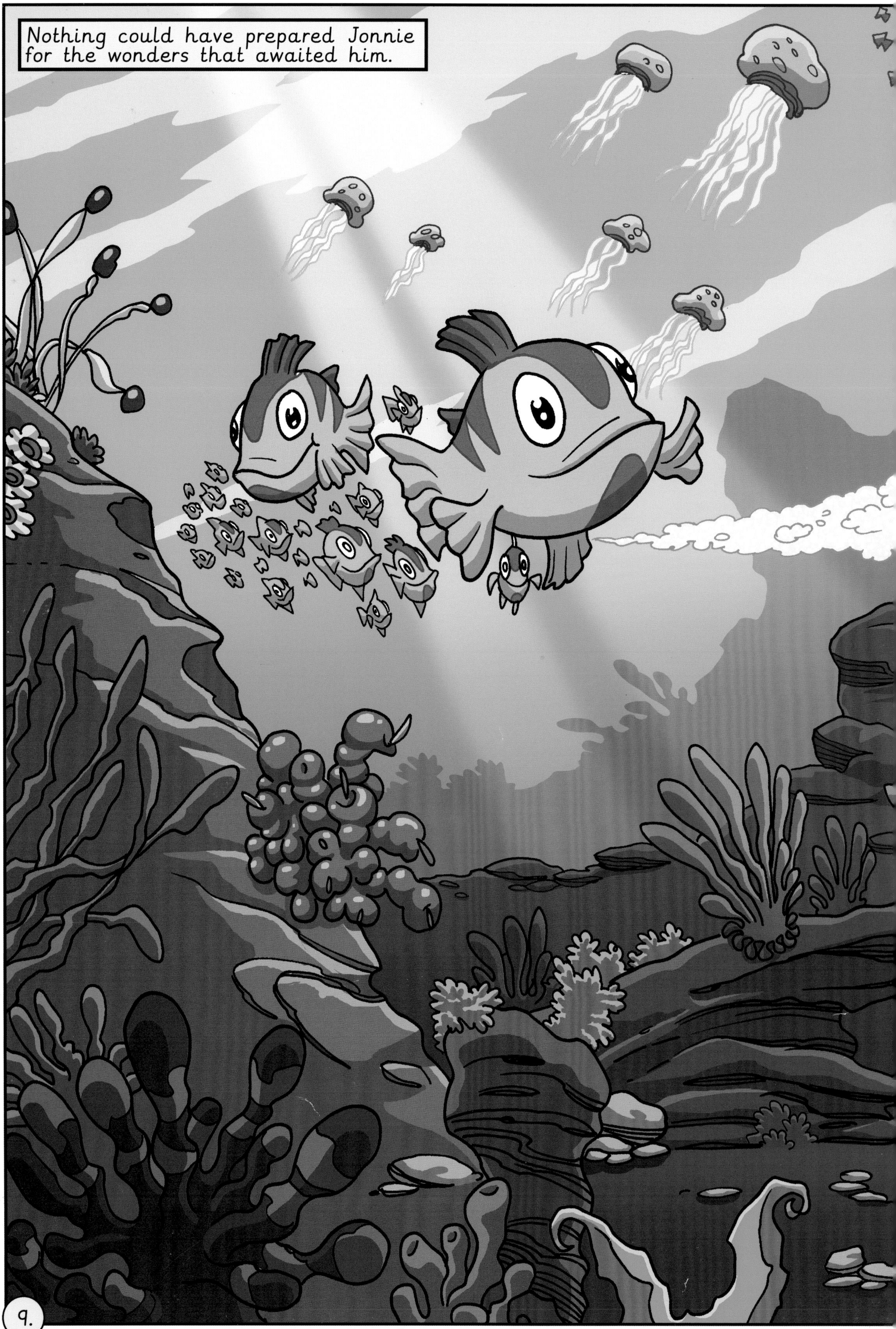
Nothing could have prepared Jonnie for the wonders that awaited him.

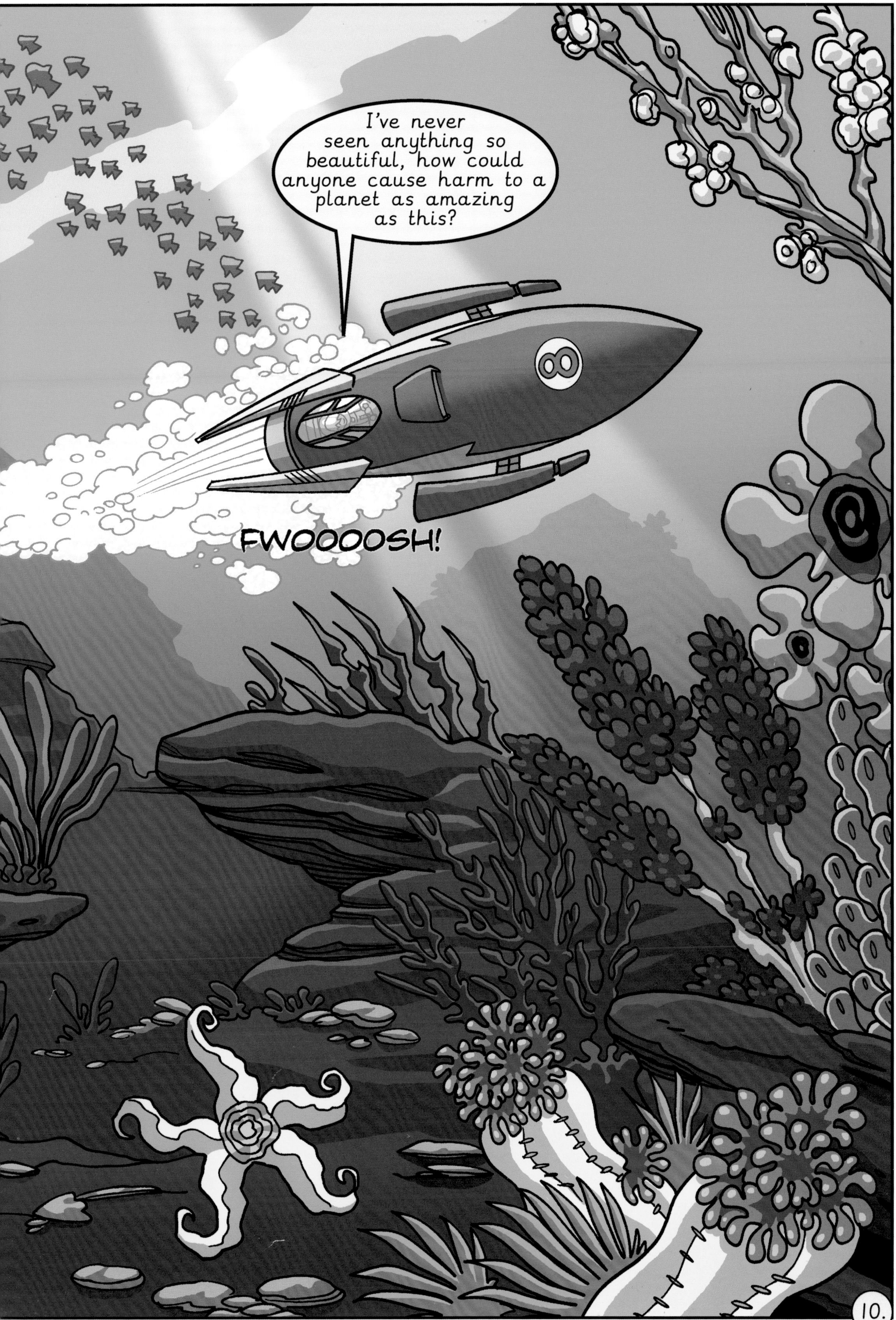
I've never seen anything so beautiful, how could anyone cause harm to a planet as amazing as this?
FWOOOOSH!

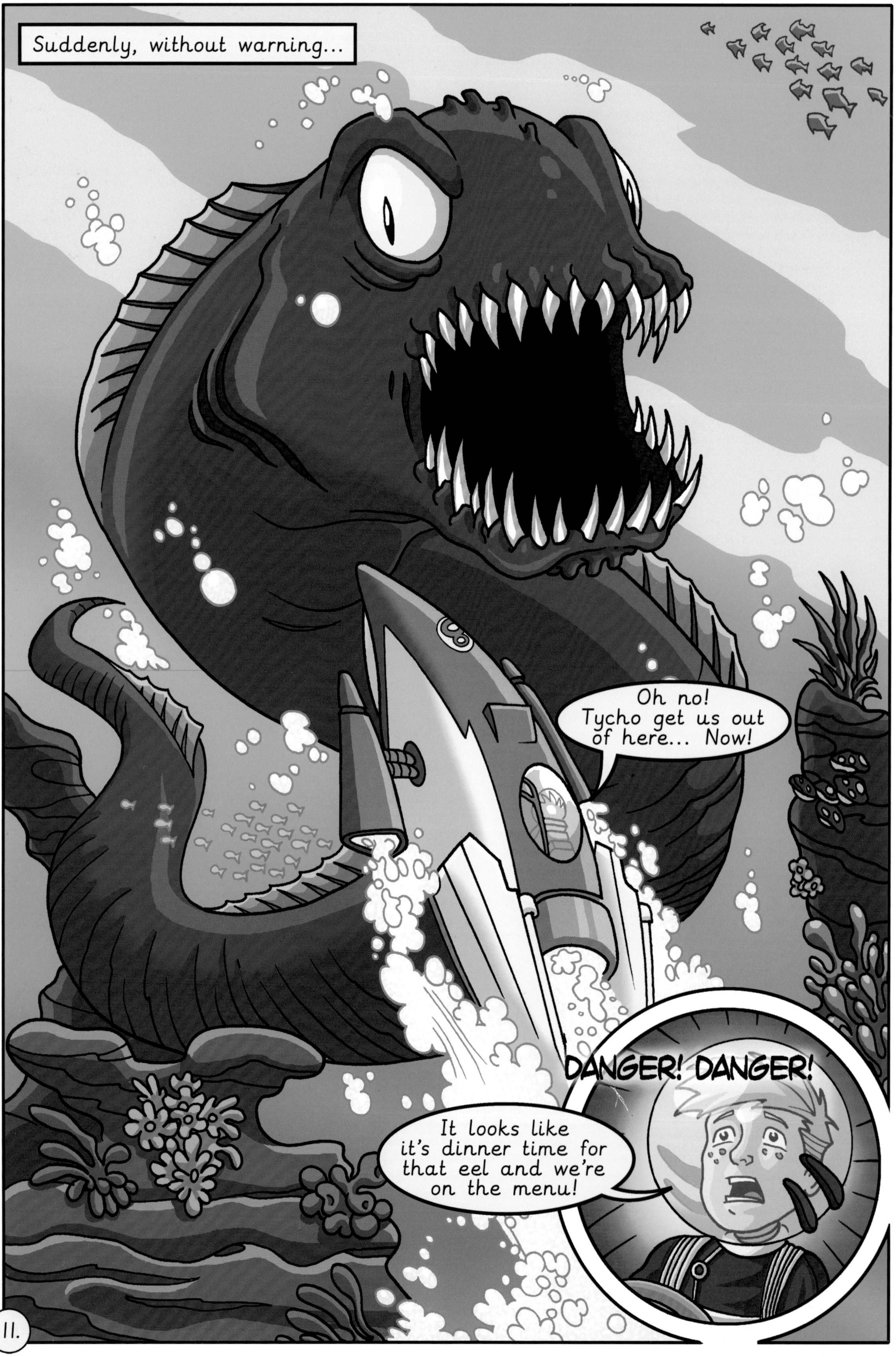
Suddenly, without warning...
Oh no! Tycho get us out of here... Now!
DANGER! DANGER!
It looks like it's dinner time for that eel and we're on the menu!

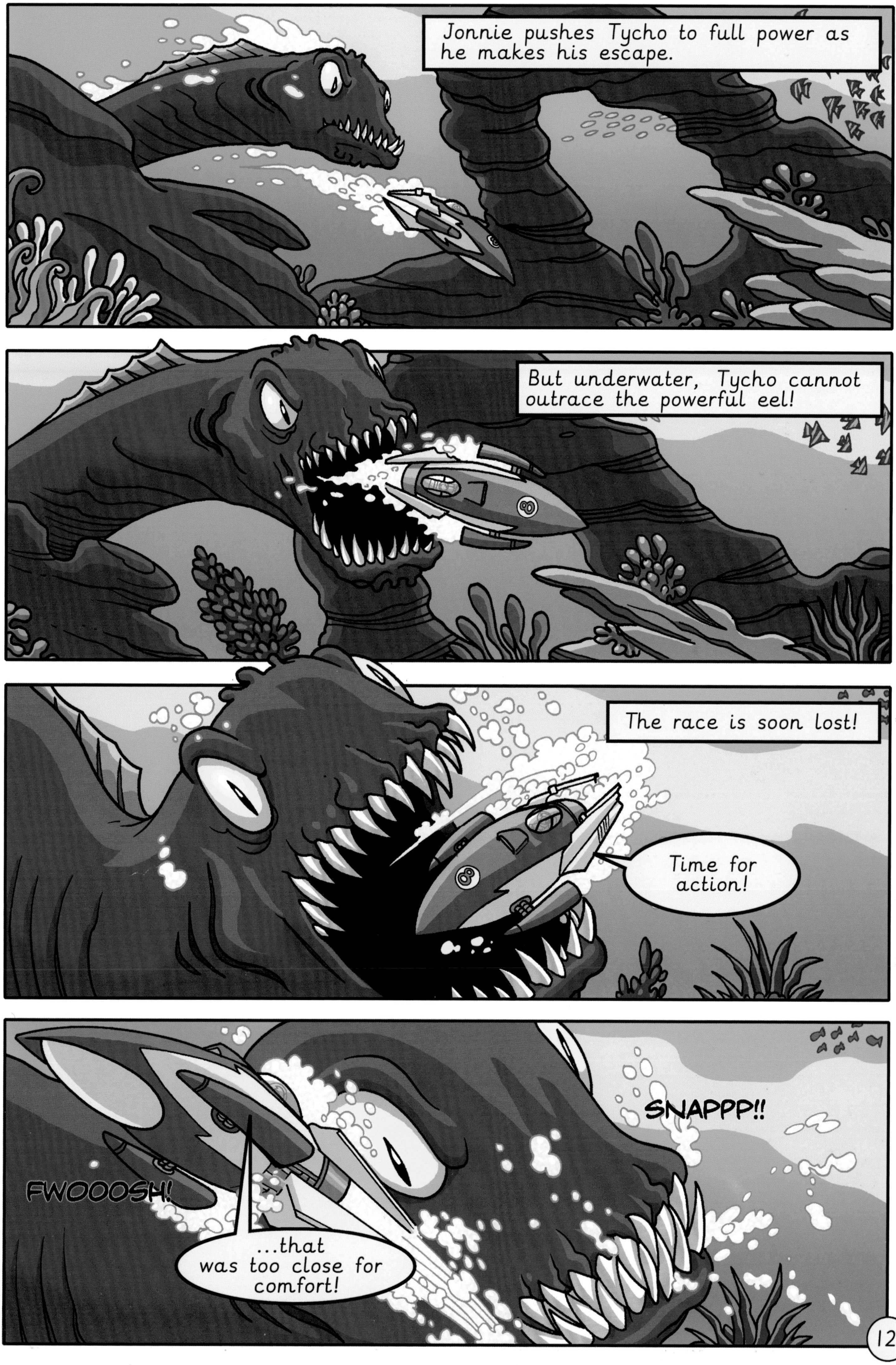
Jonnie pushes Tycho to full power as he makes his escape.
But underwater, Tycho cannot outrace the powerful eel!
The race is soon lost!
Time for action!
SNAPPP!!
FWOOOSH!
...that was too close for comfort!

Try as he might, Jonnie cannot get away.

Time for some drastic action.

I need to make this battle more even.

This should slow Jaws down, he won't be able to swim fast through this canyon.

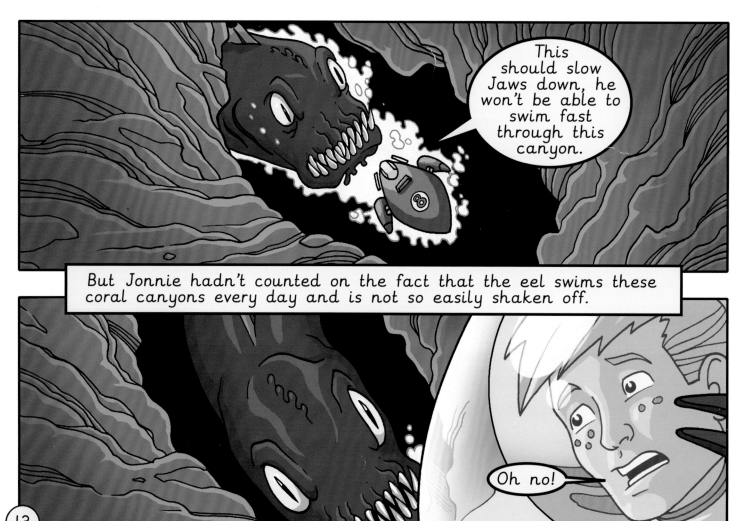

But Jonnie hadn't counted on the fact that the eel swims these coral canyons every day and is not so easily shaken off.

Oh no!

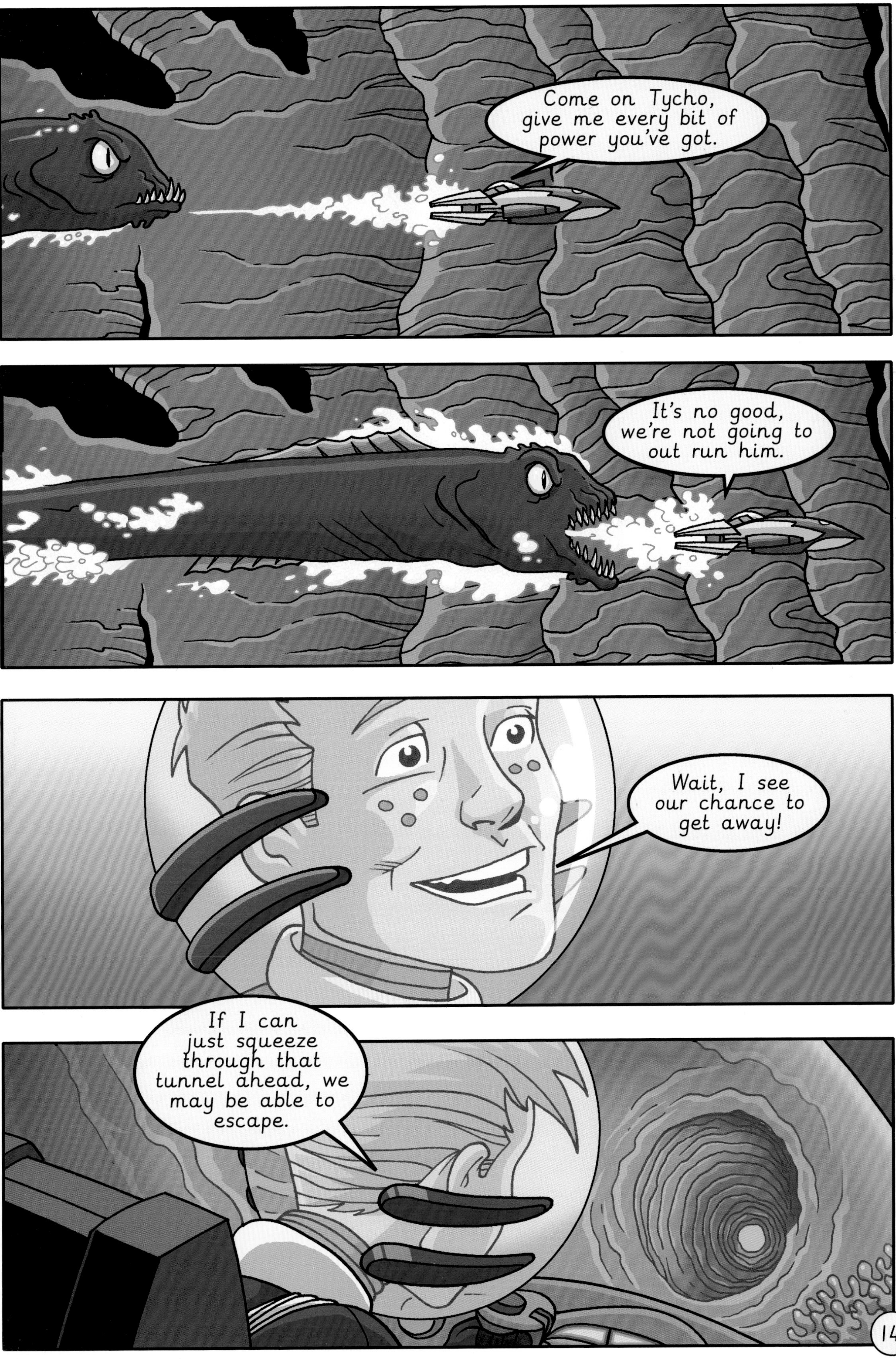
Come on Tycho, give me every bit of power you've got.
It's no good, we're not going to out run him.
Wait, I see our chance to get away!
If I can just squeeze through that tunnel ahead, we may be able to escape.

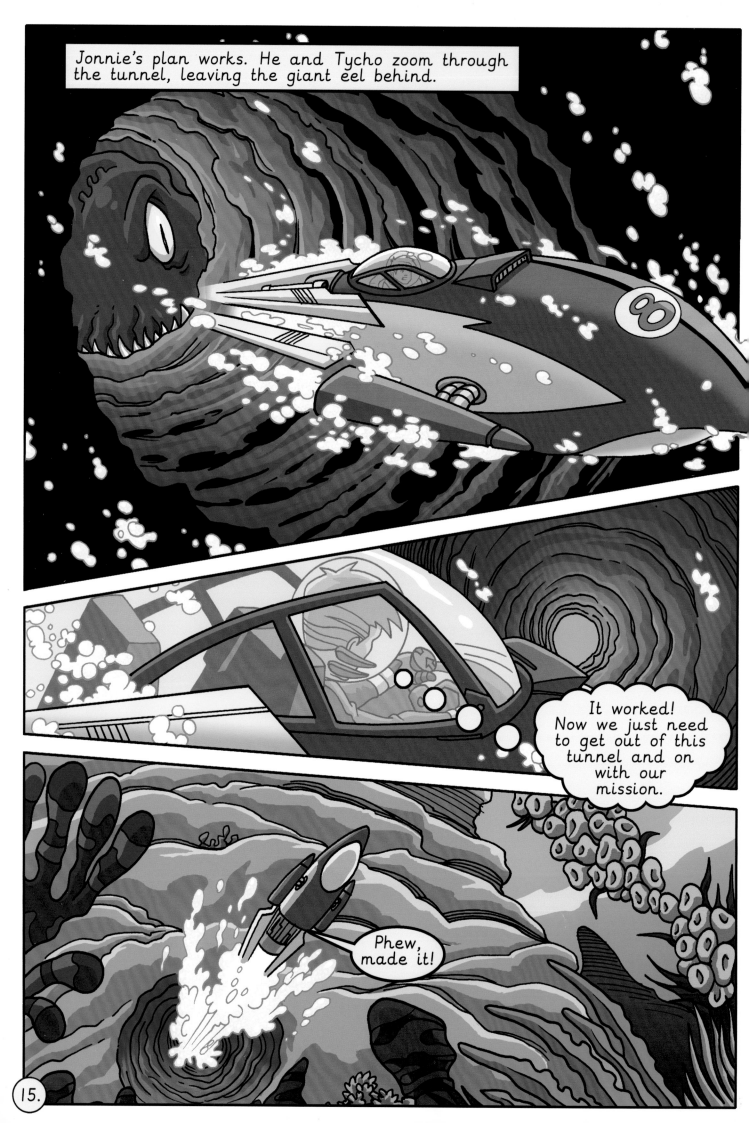

Jonnie's plan works. He and Tycho zoom through the tunnel, leaving the giant eel behind.

It worked! Now we just need to get out of this tunnel and on with our mission.

Phew, made it!

15.

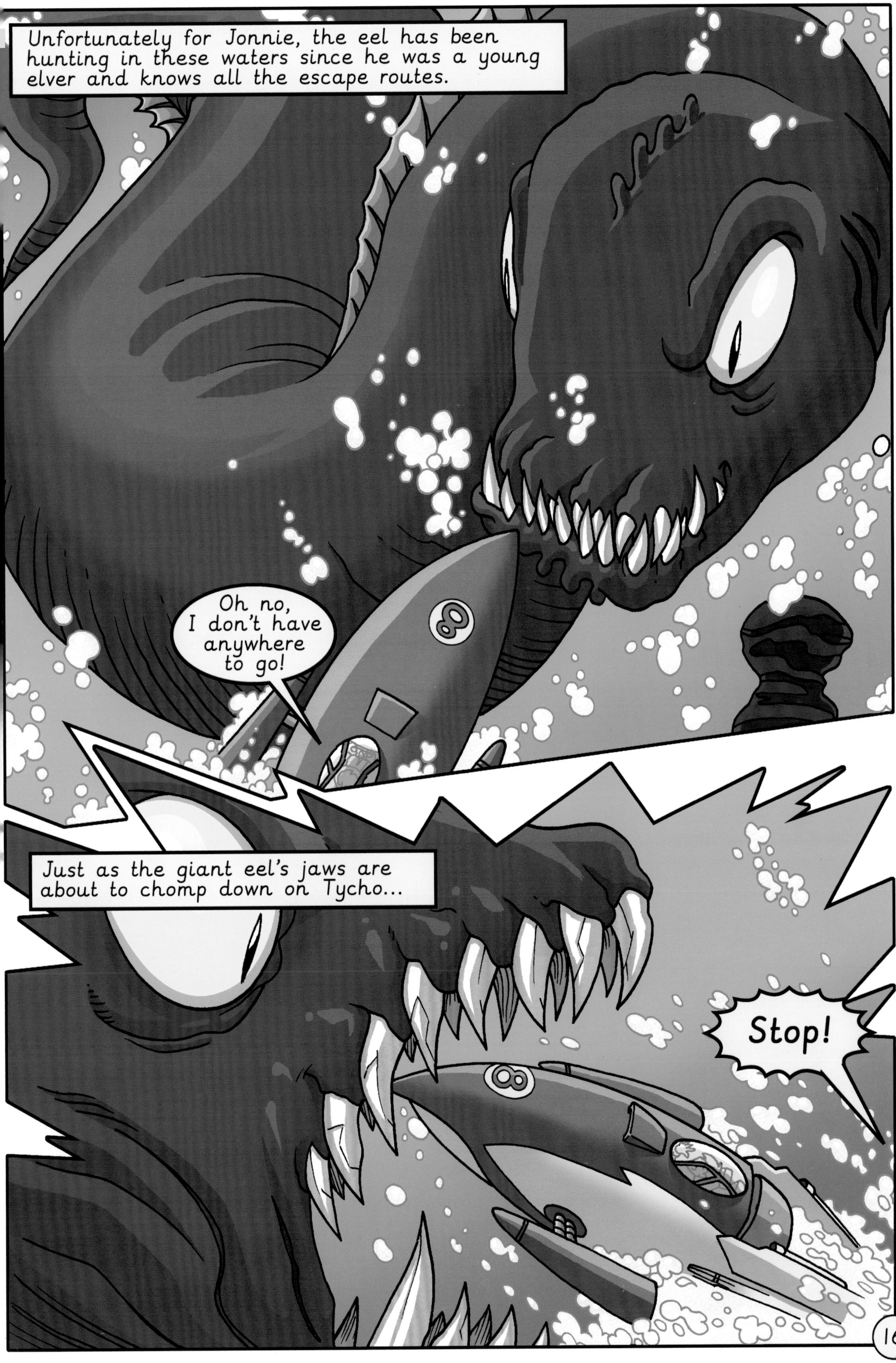
Unfortunately for Jonnie, the eel has been hunting in these waters since he was a young elver and knows all the escape routes.
Oh no, I don't have anywhere to go!
Just as the giant eel's jaws are about to chomp down on Tycho...
Stop!

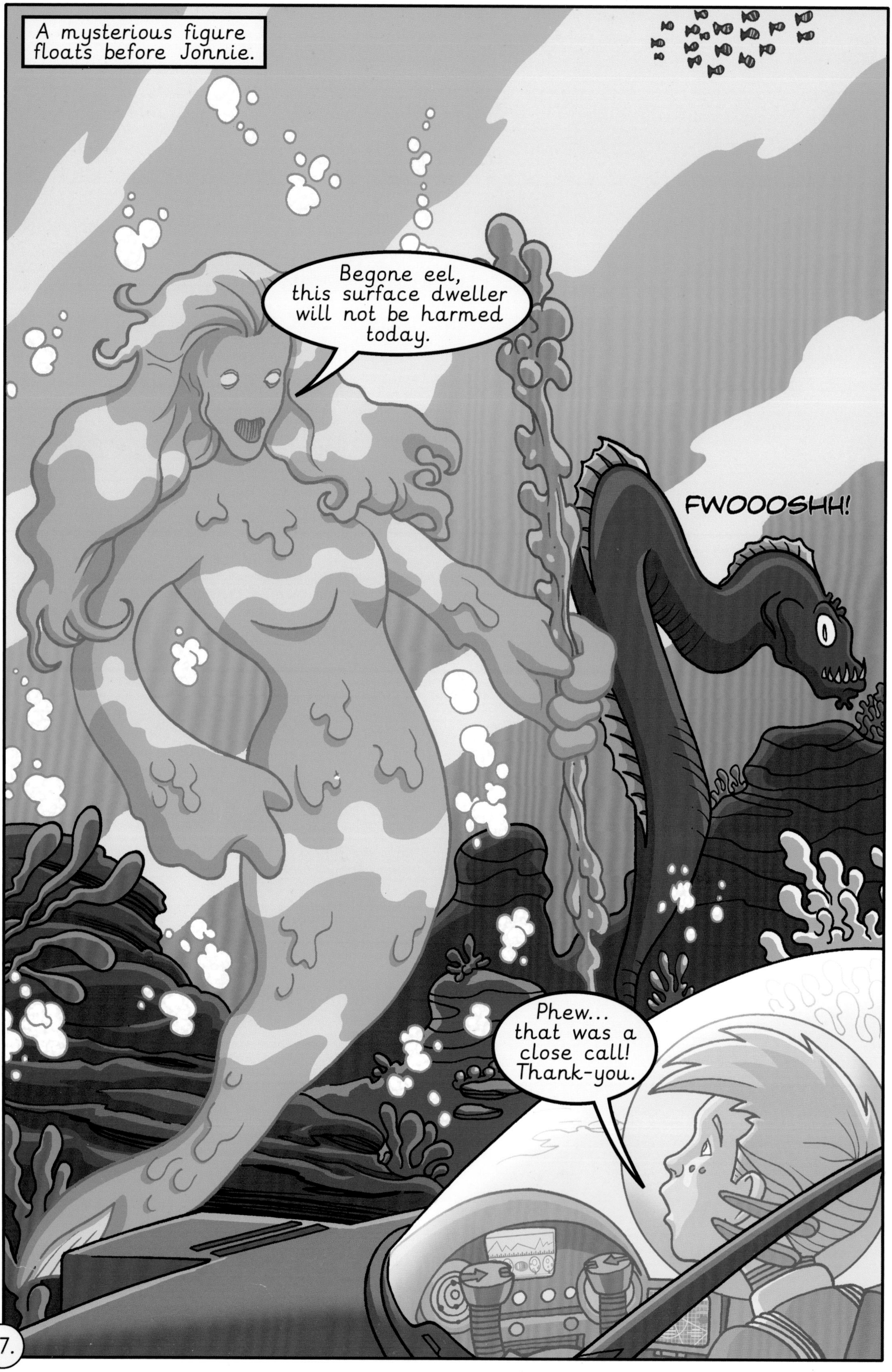
A mysterious figure floats before Jonnie.
Begone eel, this surface dweller will not be harmed today.
FWOOOSHH!
Phew... that was a close call! Thank-you.

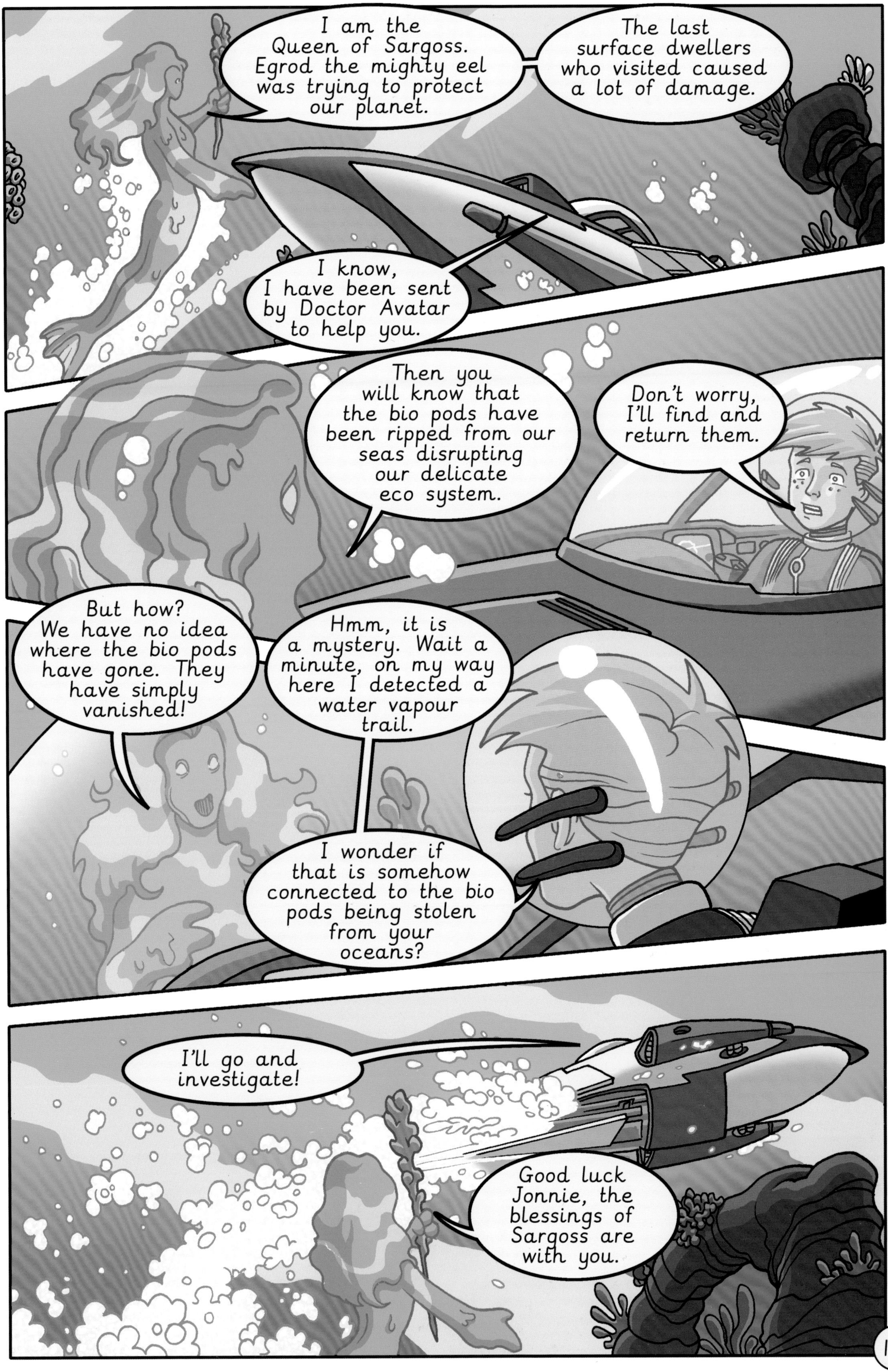
I am the Queen of Sargoss. Egrod the mighty eel was trying to protect our planet.
The last surface dwellers who visited caused a lot of damage.
I know, I have been sent by Doctor Avatar to help you.
Then you will know that the bio pods have been ripped from our seas disrupting our delicate eco system.
Don't worry, I'll find and return them.
But how? We have no idea where the bio pods have gone. They have simply vanished!
Hmm, it is a mystery. Wait a minute, on my way here I detected a water vapour trail.
I wonder if that is somehow connected to the bio pods being stolen from your oceans?
I'll go and investigate!
Good luck Jonnie, the blessings of Sargoss are with you.

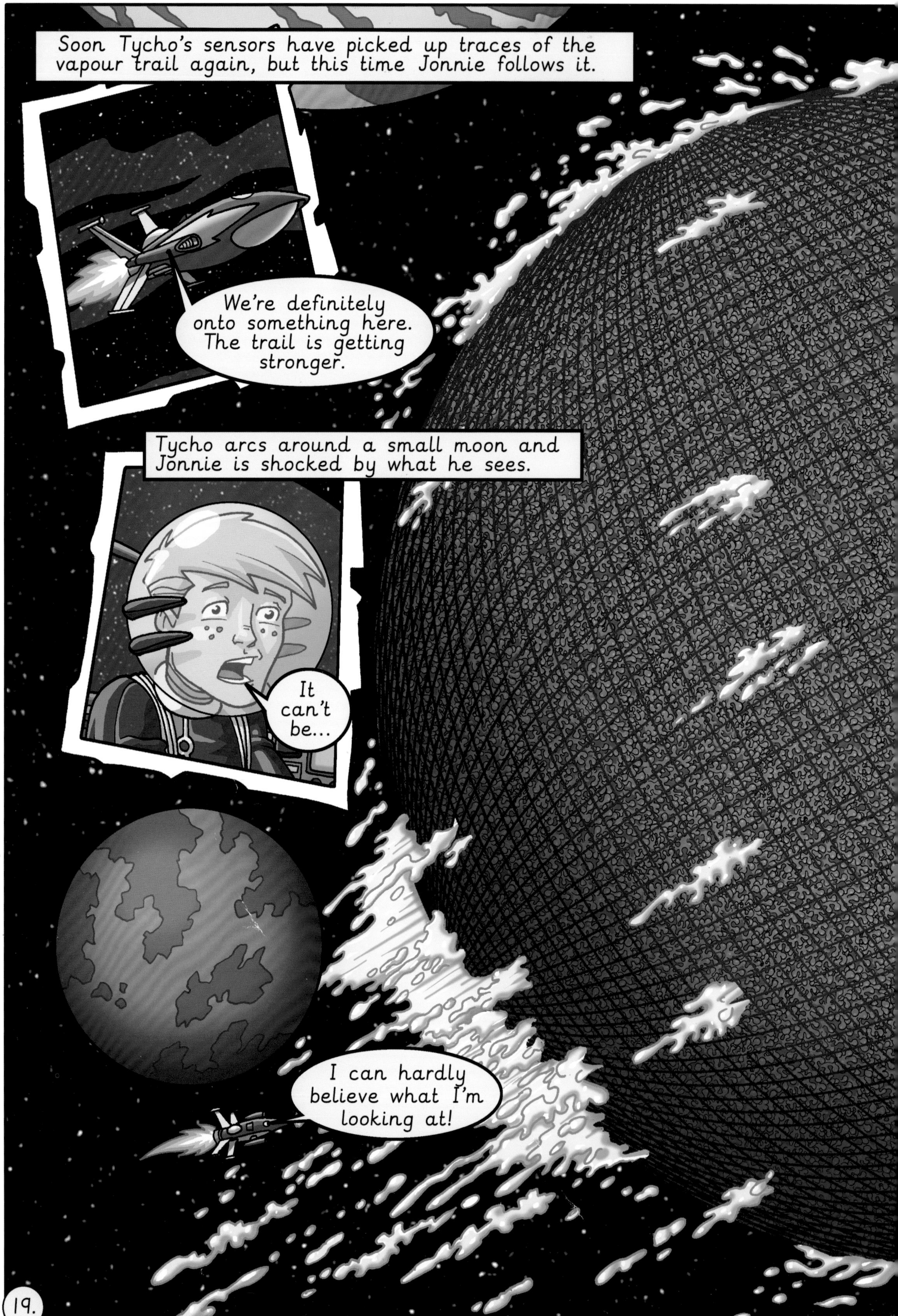

Soon Tycho's sensors have picked up traces of the vapour trail again, but this time Jonnie follows it.
We're definitely onto something here. The trail is getting stronger.
Tycho arcs around a small moon and Jonnie is shocked by what he sees.
It can't be...
I can hardly believe what I'm looking at!

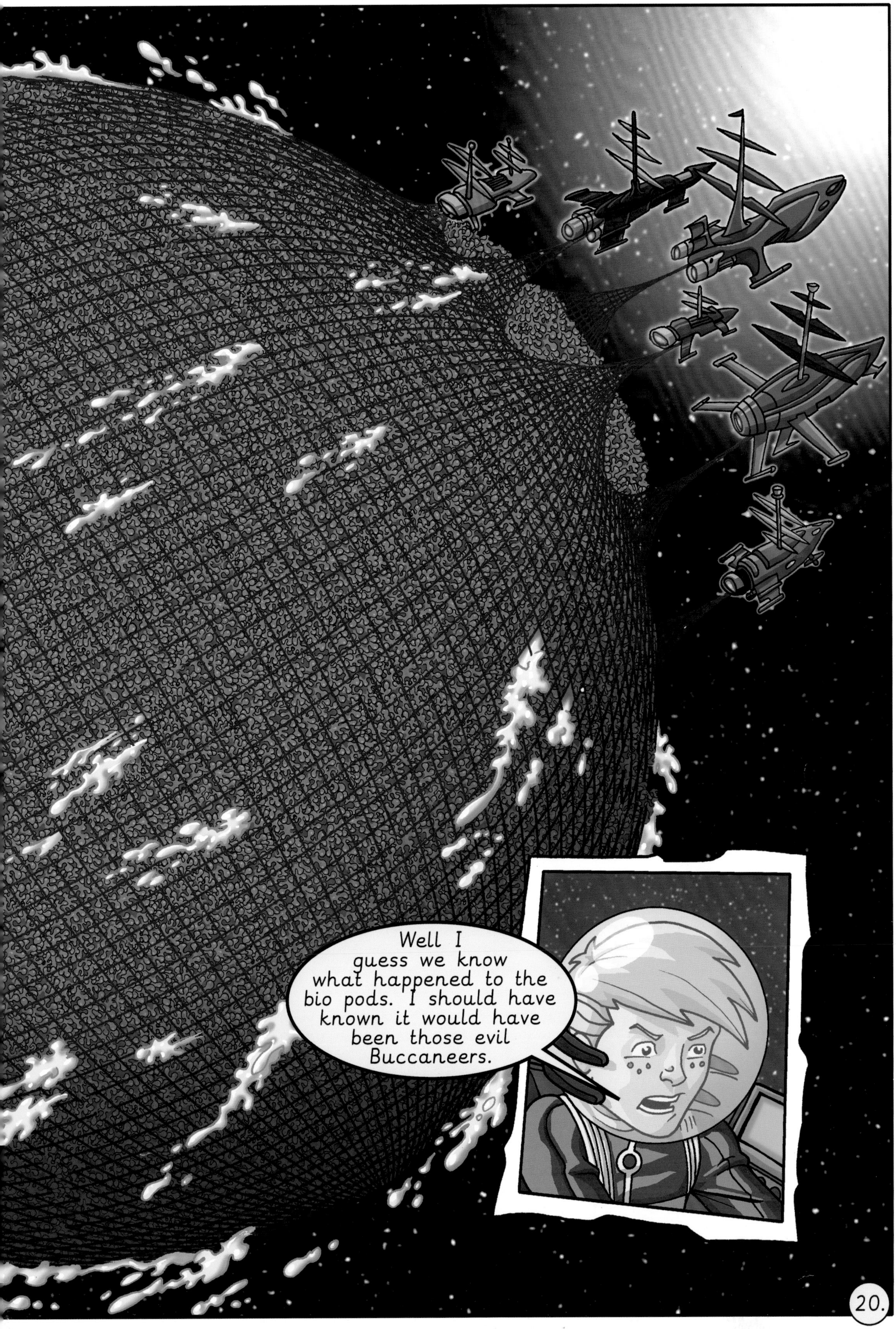
Well I guess we know what happened to the bio pods. I should have known it would have been those evil Buccaneers.

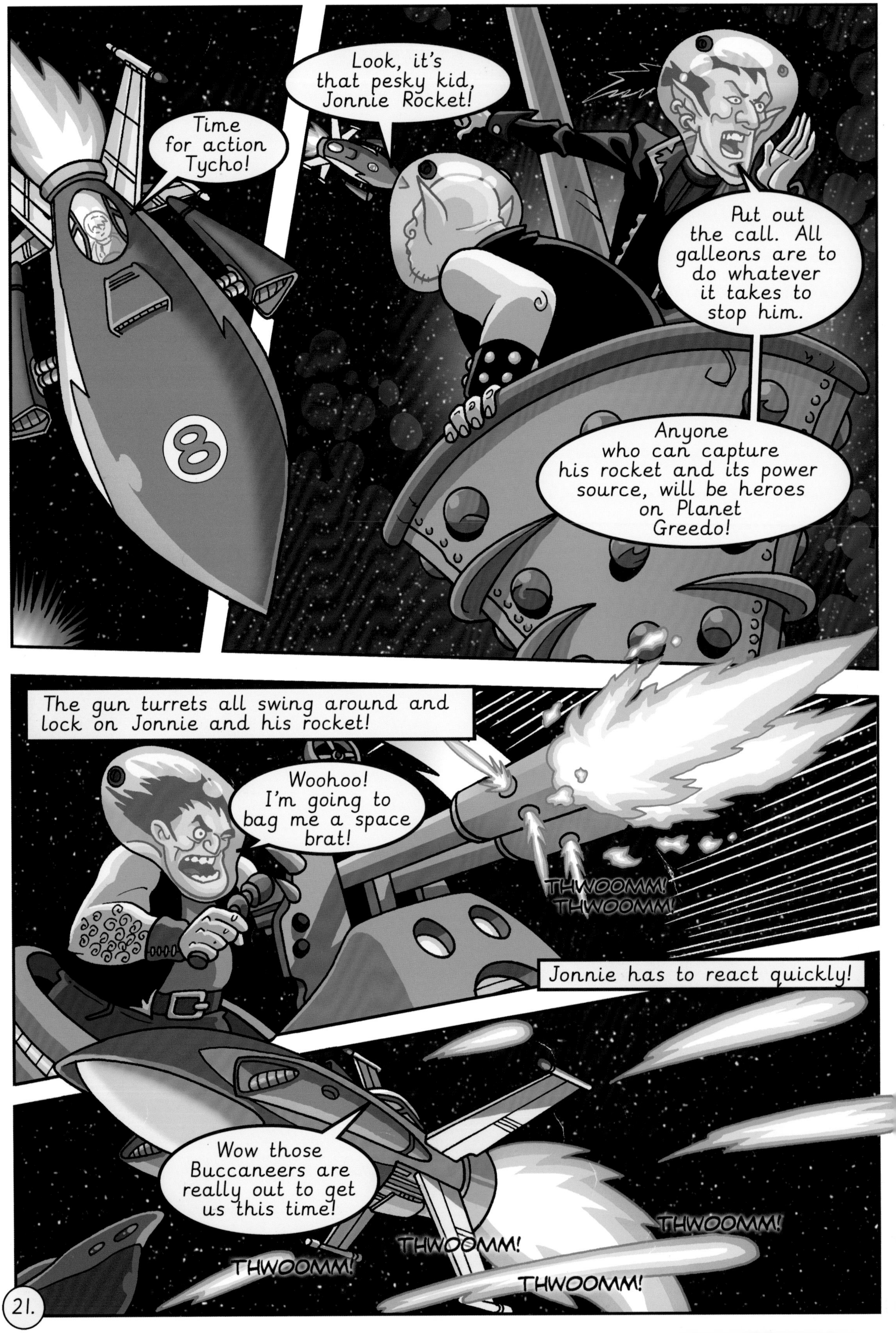
Time for action Tycho!
Look, it's that pesky kid, Jonnie Rocket!
Put out the call. All galleons are to do whatever it takes to stop him.
Anyone who can capture his rocket and its power source, will be heroes on Planet Greedo!
The gun turrets all swing around and lock on Jonnie and his rocket!
Woohoo! I'm going to bag me a space brat!
THWOOMM! THWOOMM!
Jonnie has to react quickly!
Wow those Buccaneers are really out to get us this time!
THWOOMM!
THWOOMM!
THWOOMM!
THWOOMM!

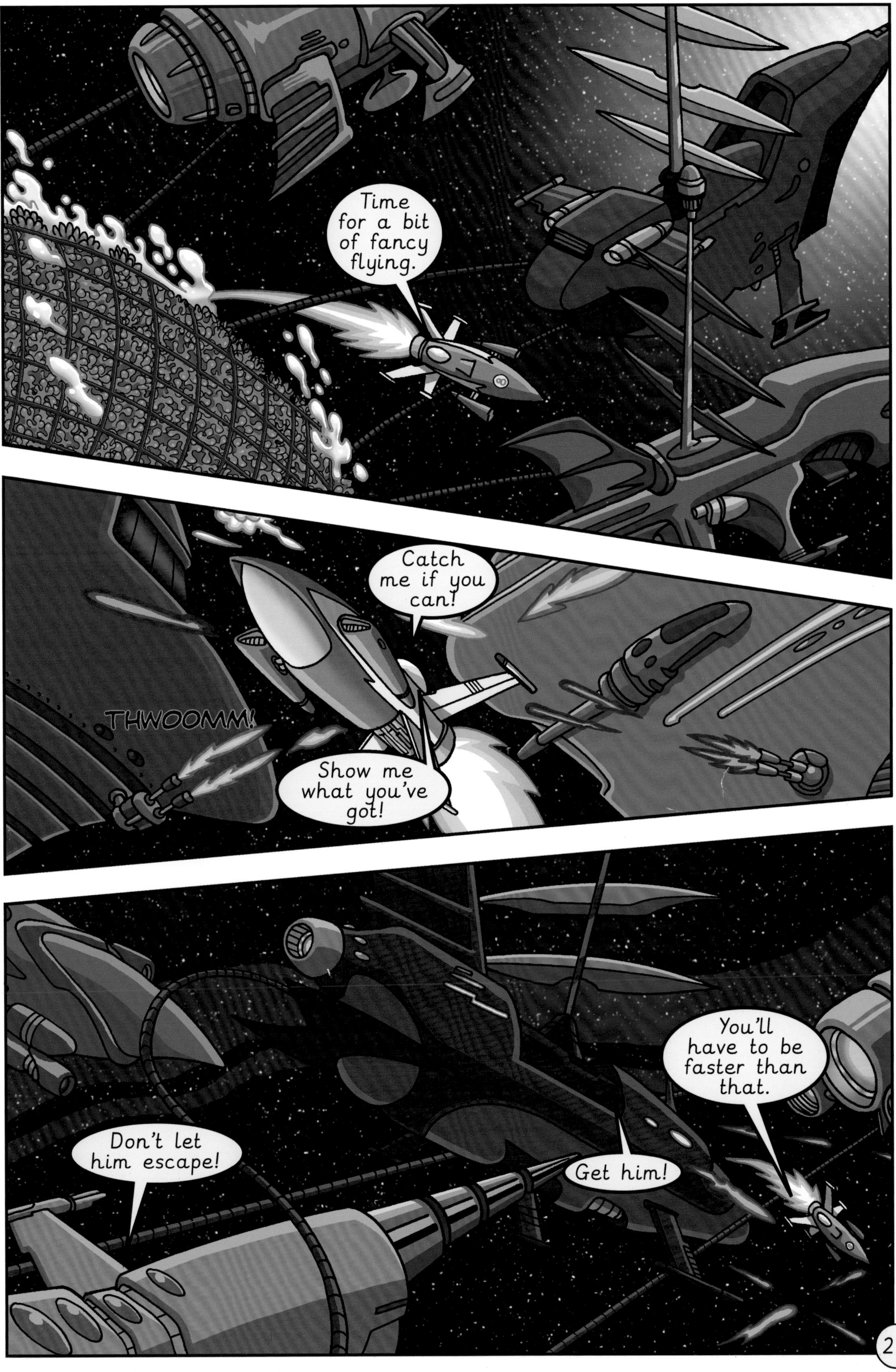

Time for a bit of fancy flying.
Catch me if you can!
THWOOMM!
Show me what you've got!
You'll have to be faster than that.
Get him!
Don't let him escape!

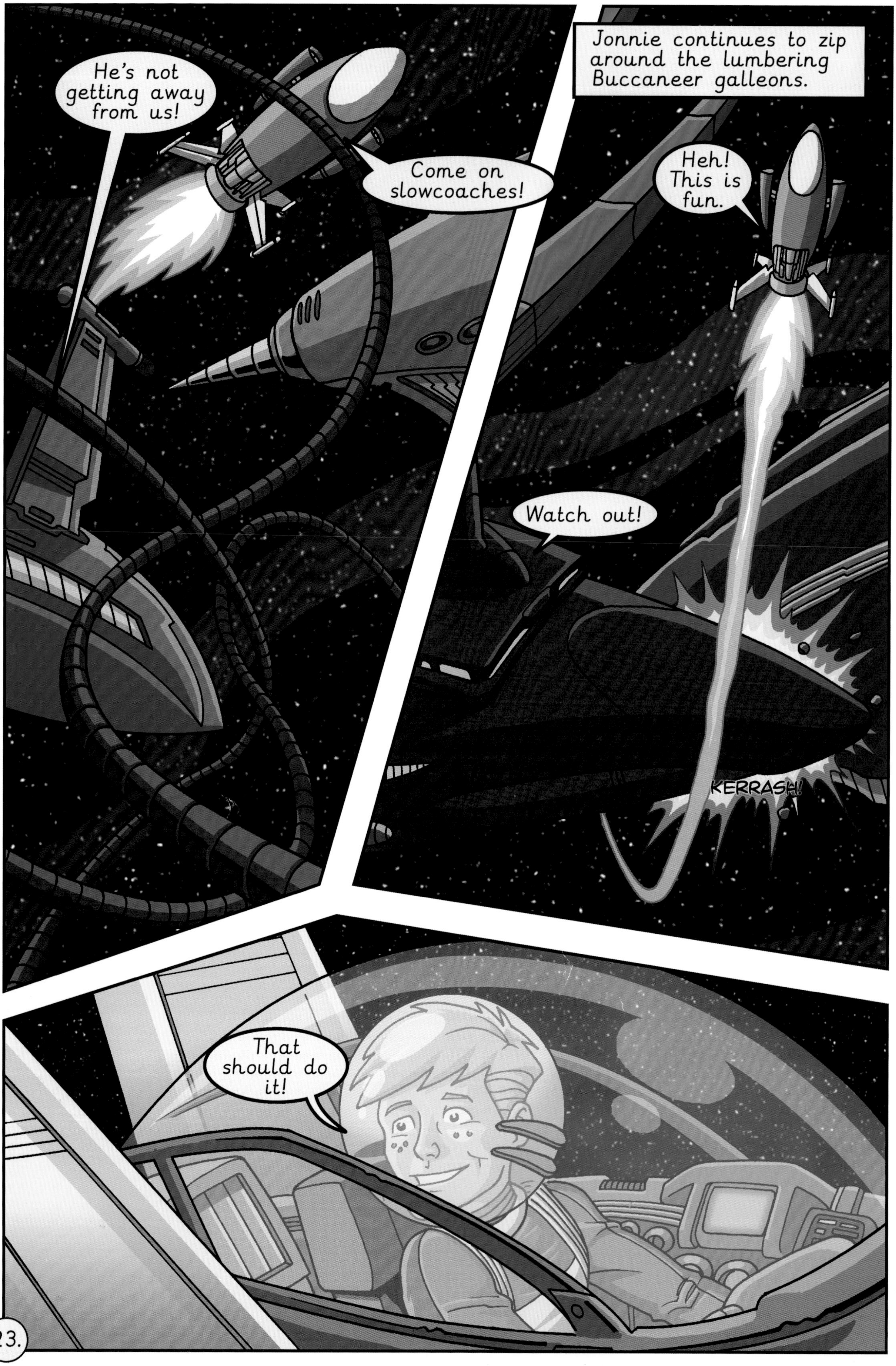
He's not getting away from us!
Come on slowcoaches!
Jonnie continues to zip around the lumbering Buccaneer galleons.
Heh! This is fun.
Watch out!
KERRASH!
That should do it!

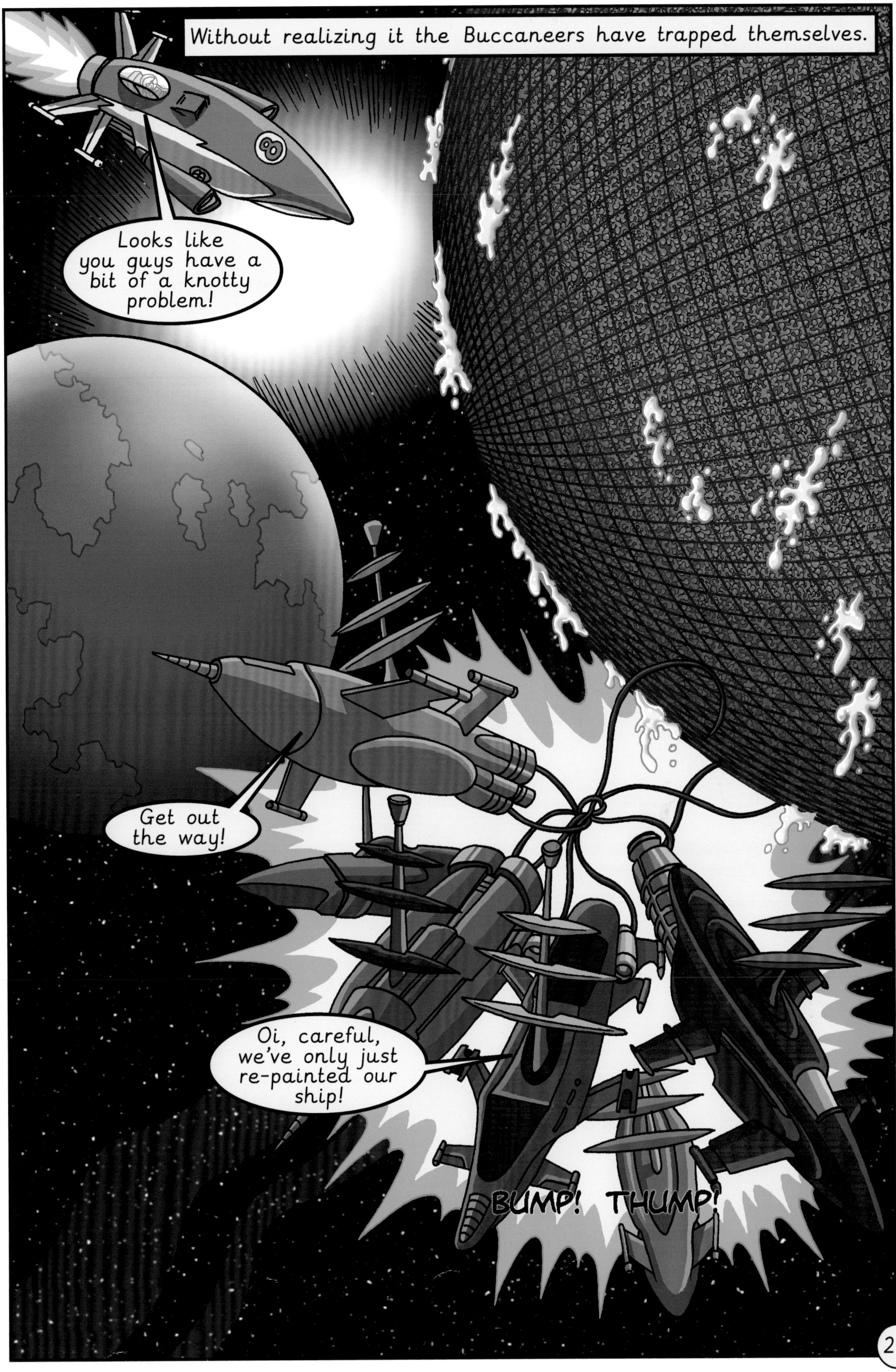
Without realizing it the Buccaneers have trapped themselves.
Looks like you guys have a bit of a knotty problem!
Get out the way!
Oi, careful, we've only just re-painted our ship!
BUMP! THUMP!

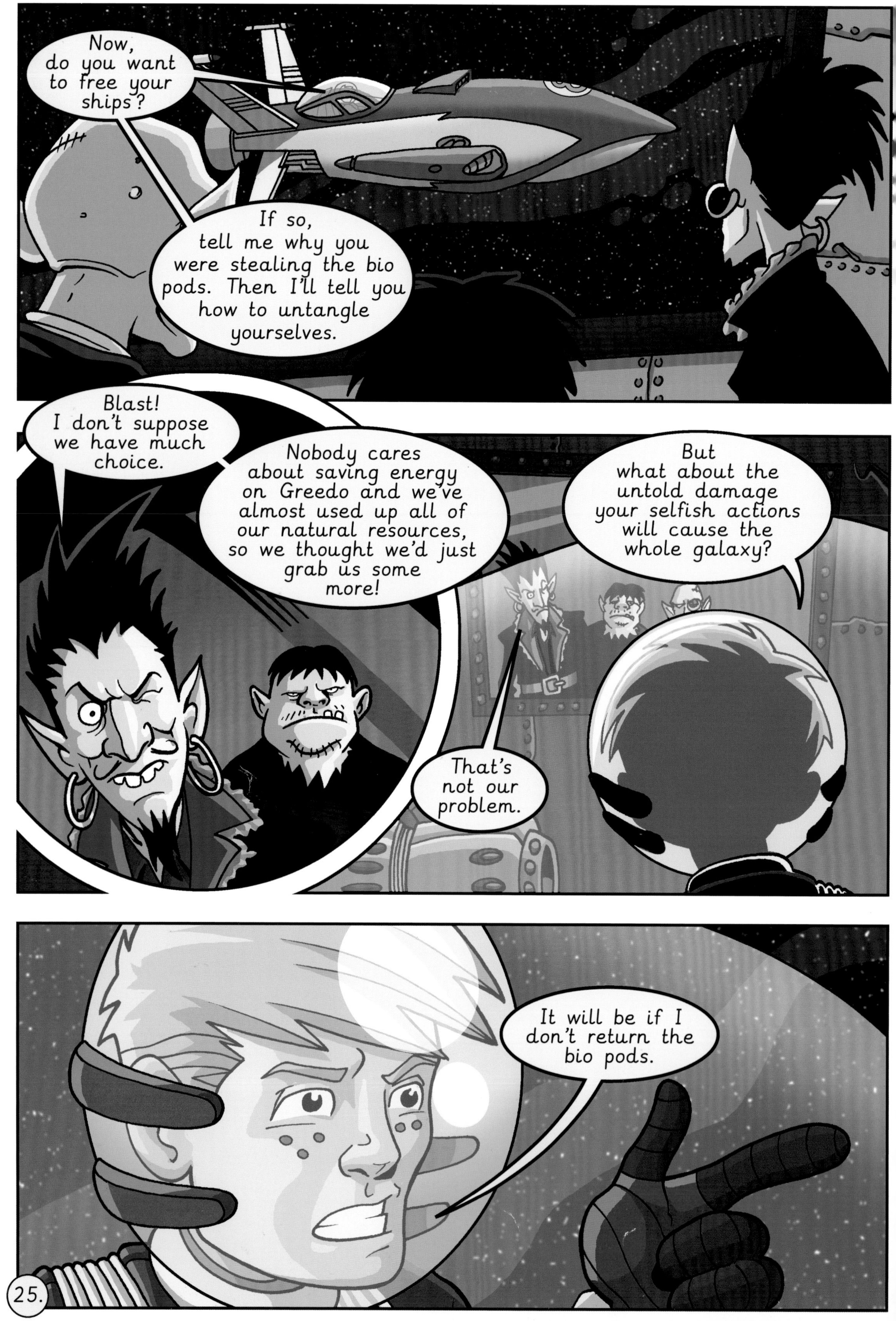
Now, do you want to free your ships?
If so, tell me why you were stealing the bio pods. Then I'll tell you how to untangle yourselves.
Blast! I don't suppose we have much choice.
Nobody cares about saving energy on Greedo and we've almost used up all of our natural resources, so we thought we'd just grab us some more!
But what about the untold damage your selfish actions will cause the whole galaxy?
That's not our problem.
It will be if I don't return the bio pods.

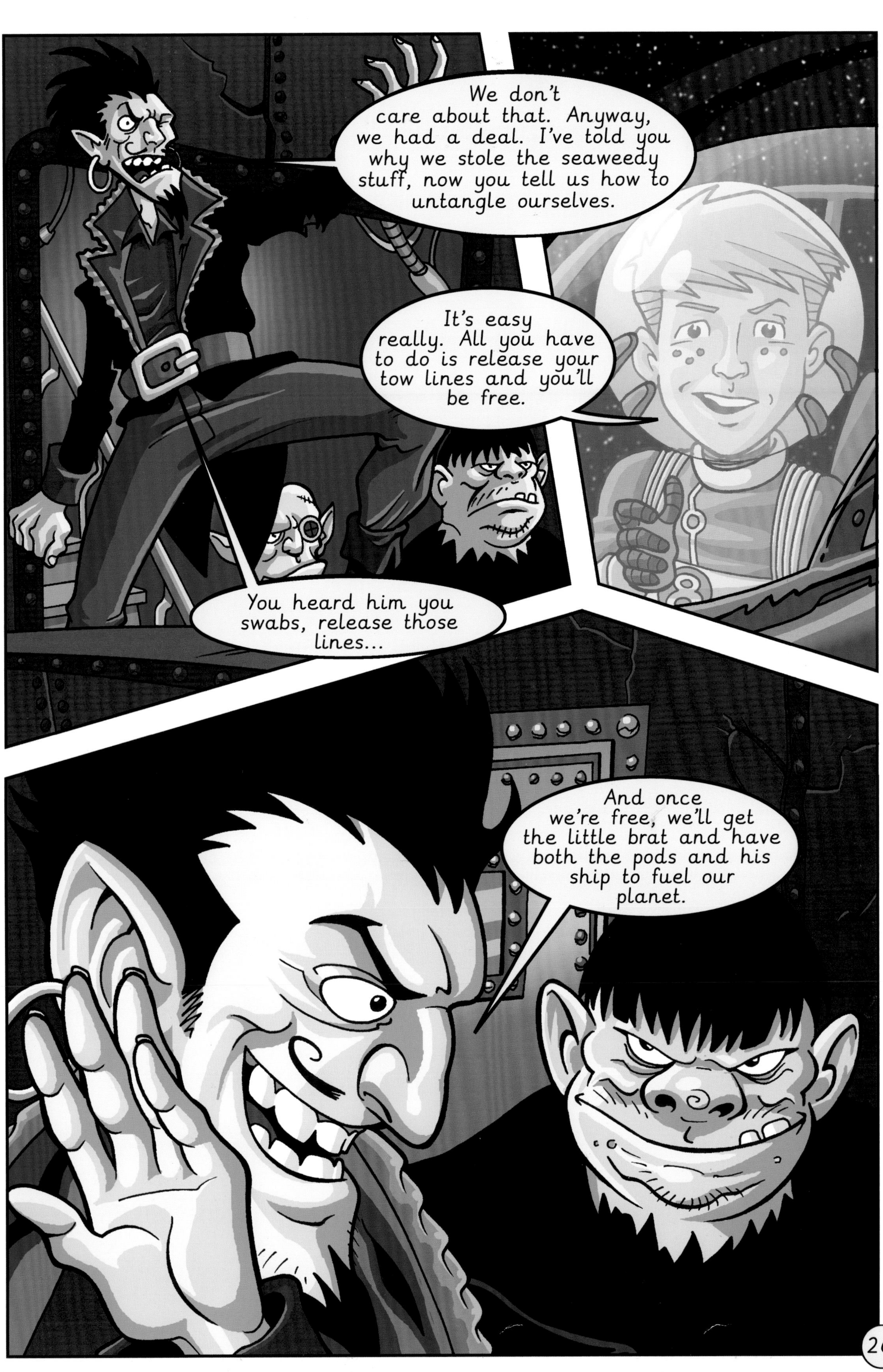
We don't care about that. Anyway, we had a deal. I've told you why we stole the seaweedy stuff, now you tell us how to untangle ourselves.
It's easy really. All you have to do is release your tow lines and you'll be free.
You heard him you swabs, release those lines...
And once we're free, we'll get the little brat and have both the pods and his ship to fuel our planet.

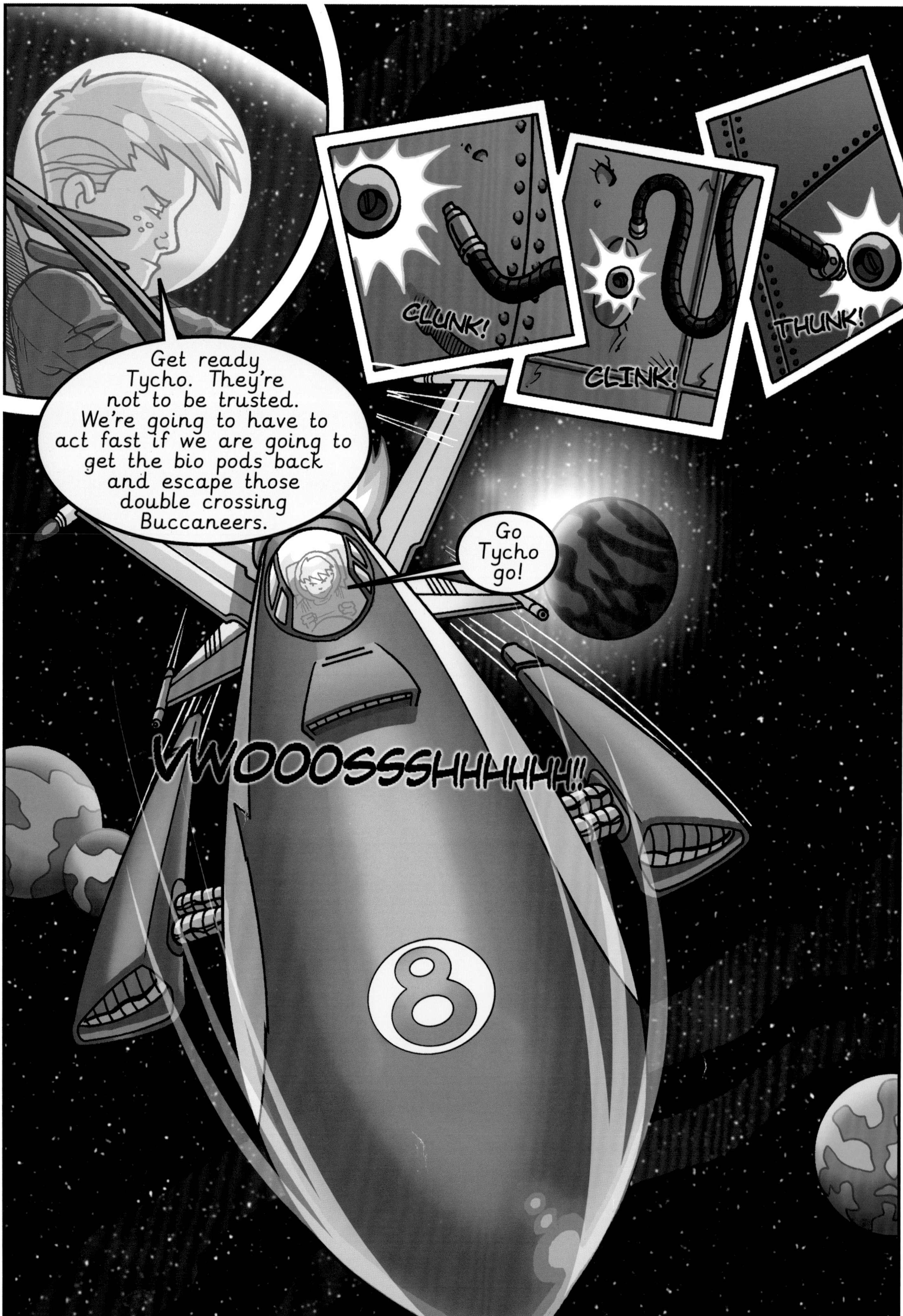
CLUNK!
CLINK!
THUNK!
Get ready Tycho. They're not to be trusted. We're going to have to act fast if we are going to get the bio pods back and escape those double crossing Buccaneers.
Go Tycho go!
VWOOOSSSHHHHHH!!
8

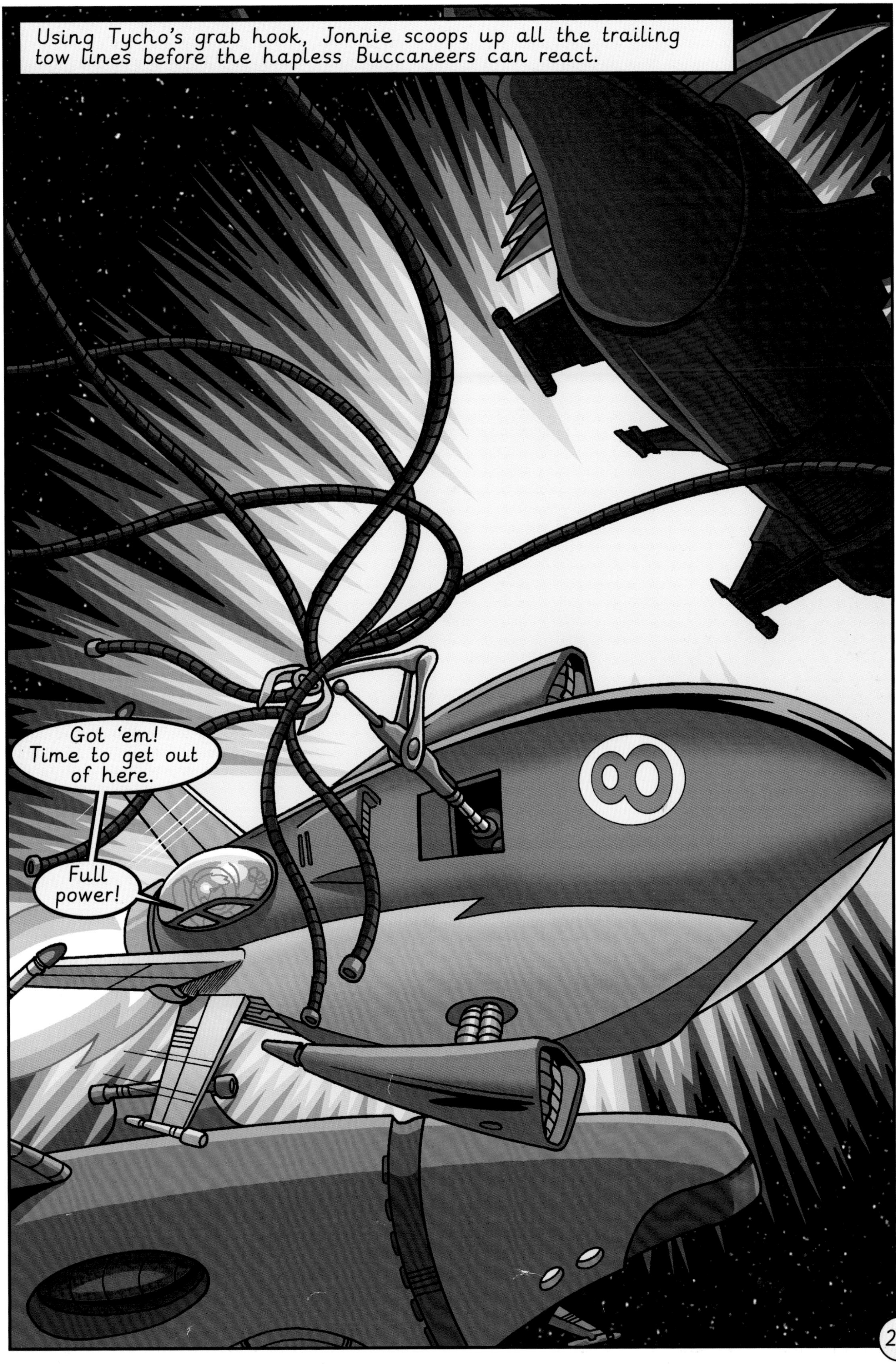
Using Tycho's grab hook, Jonnie scoops up all the trailing tow lines before the hapless Buccaneers can react.
Got 'em! Time to get out of here.
Full power!

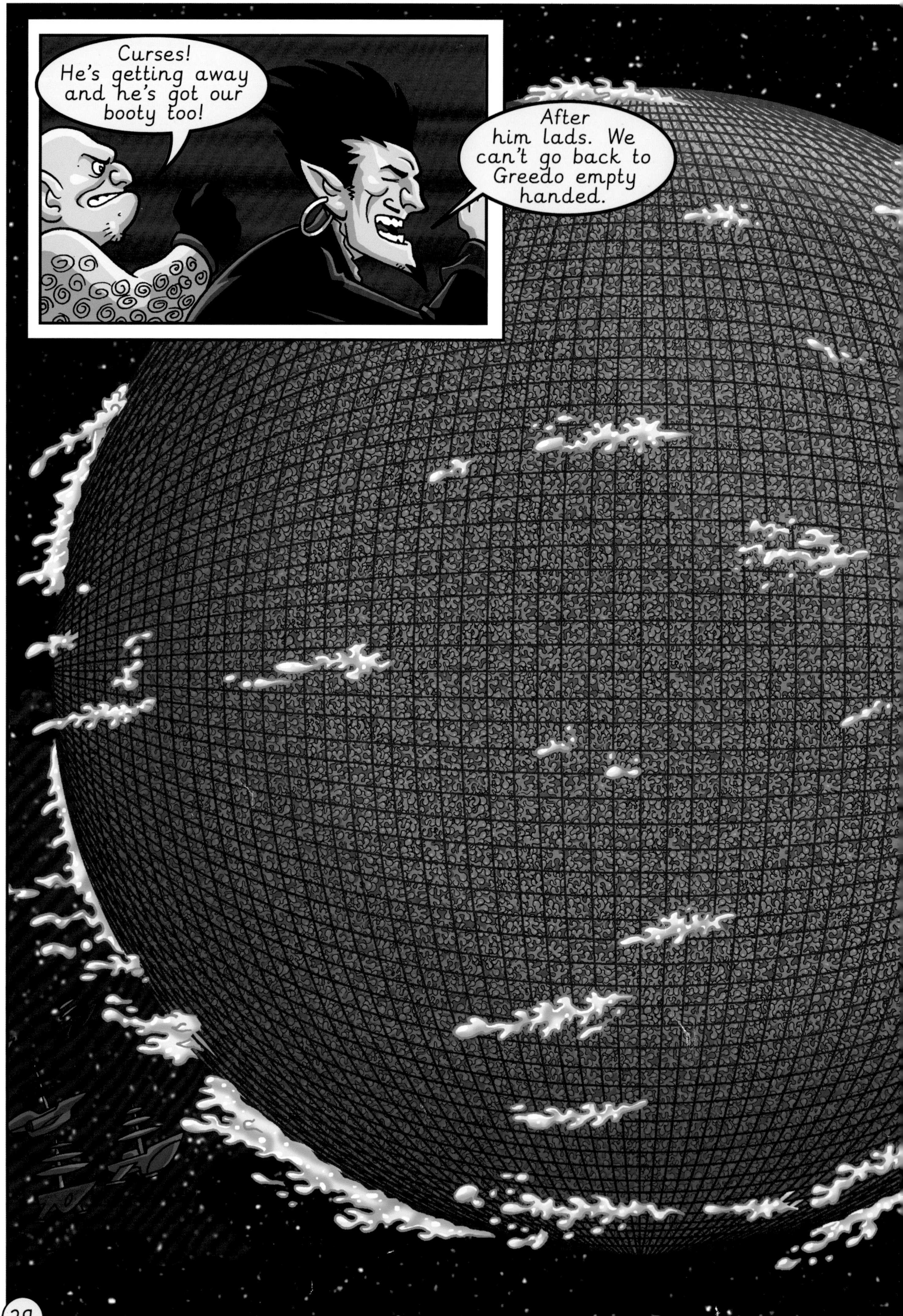
Curses! He's getting away and he's got our booty too!
After him lads. We can't go back to Greedo empty handed.

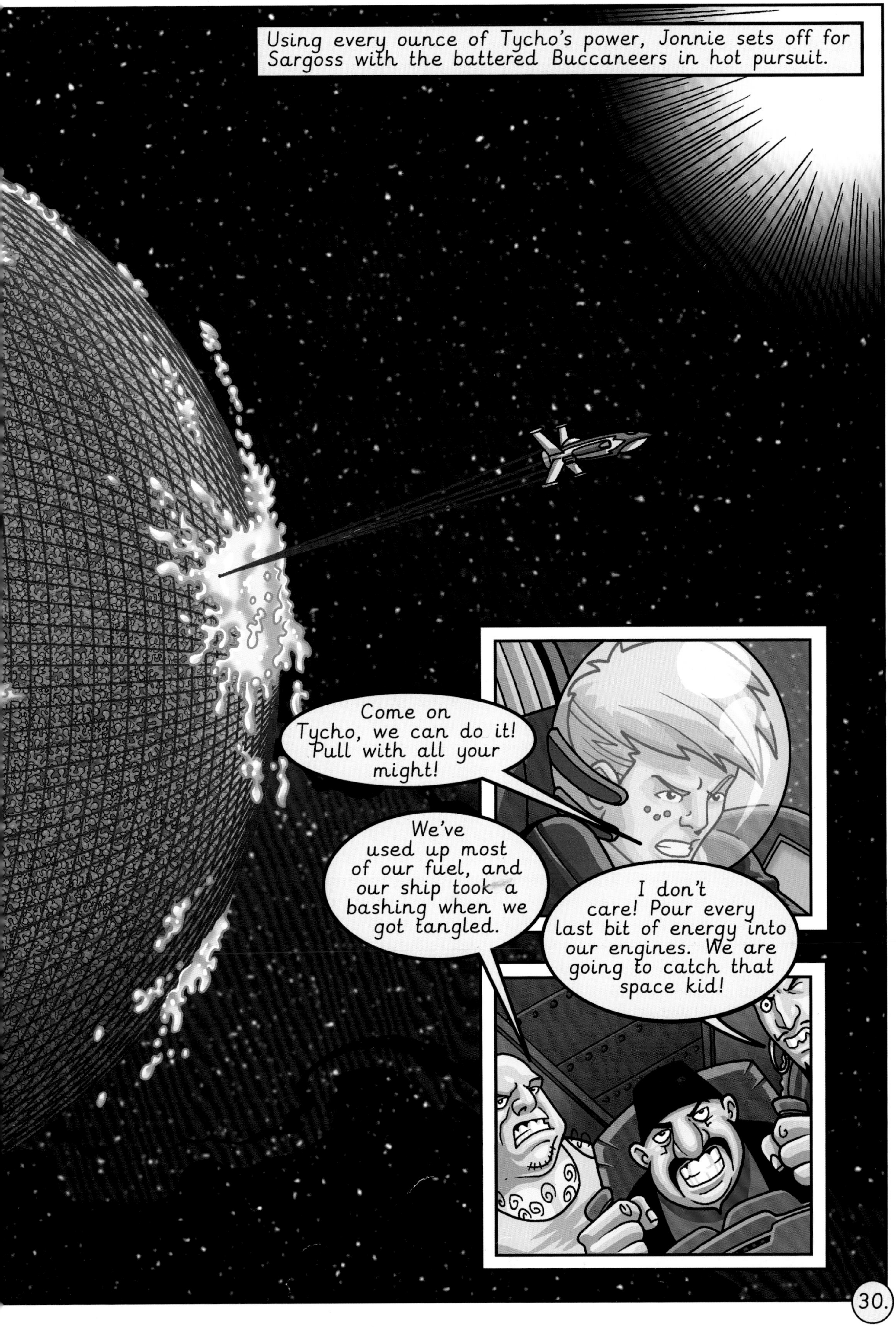
Using every ounce of Tycho's power, Jonnie sets off for Sargoss with the battered Buccaneers in hot pursuit.
Come on Tycho, we can do it! Pull with all your might!
We've used up most of our fuel, and our ship took a bashing when we got tangled.
I don't care! Pour every last bit of energy into our engines. We are going to catch that space kid!

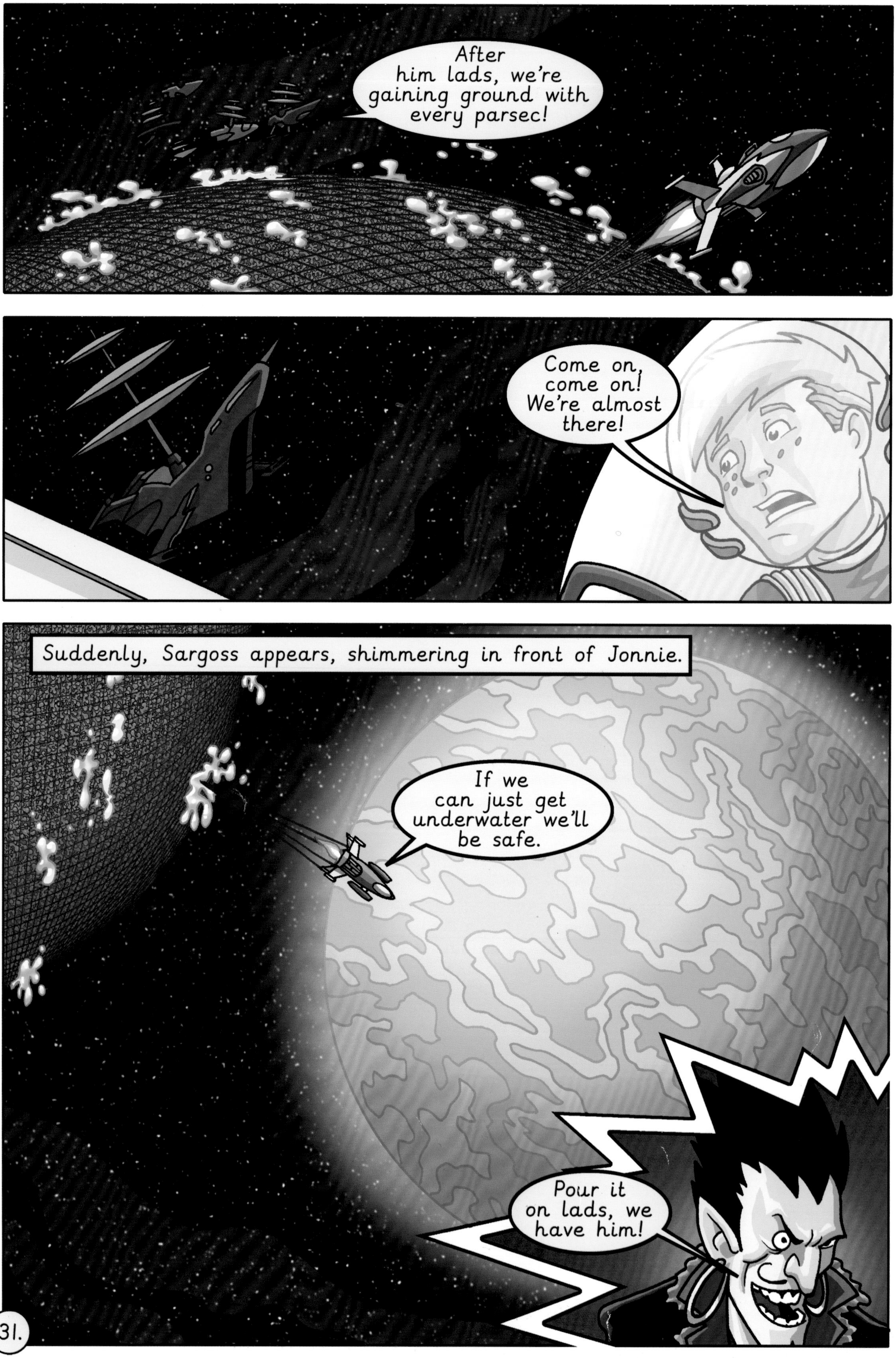
After him lads, we're gaining ground with every parsec!
Come on, come on! We're almost there!
Suddenly, Sargoss appears, shimmering in front of Jonnie.
If we can just get underwater we'll be safe.
Pour it on lads, we have him!

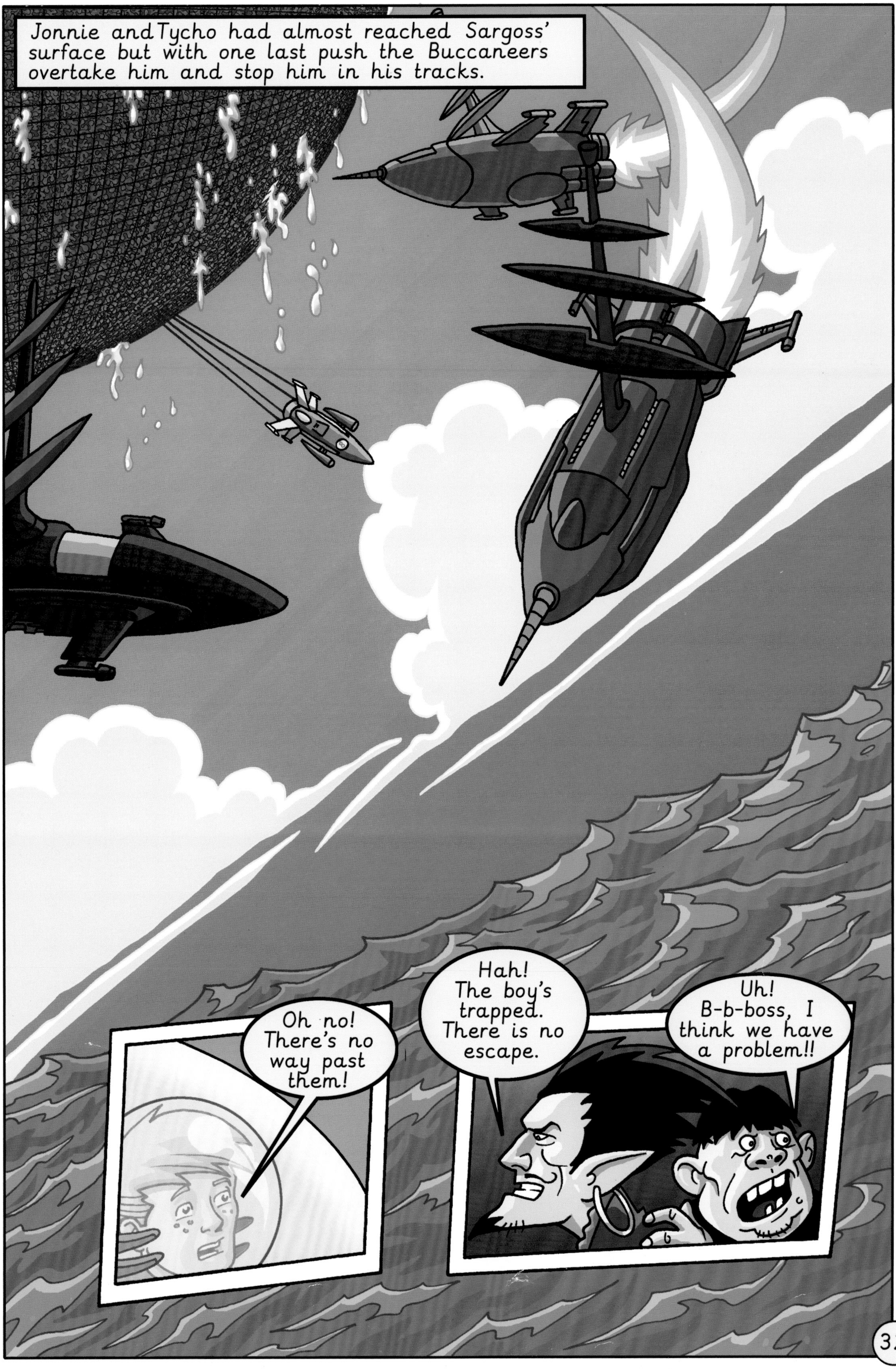
Jonnie and Tycho had almost reached Sargoss' surface but with one last push the Buccaneers overtake him and stop him in his tracks.
Oh no! There's no way past them!
Hah! The boy's trapped. There is no escape.
Uh! B-b-boss, I think we have a problem!!

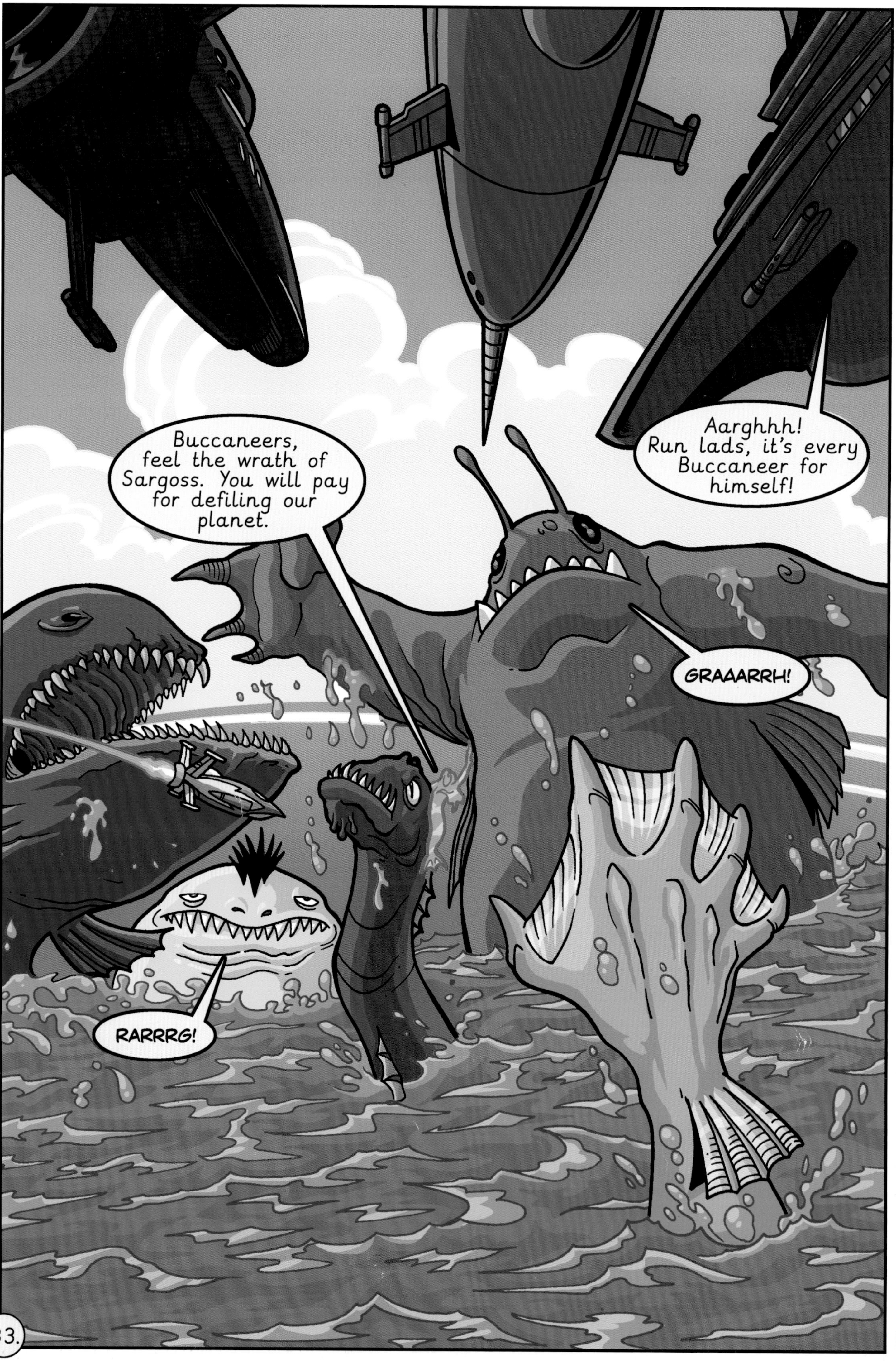
Buccaneers, feel the wrath of Sargoss. You will pay for defiling our planet.
Aarghhh! Run lads, it's every Buccaneer for himself!
GRAAARRH!
RARRRG!

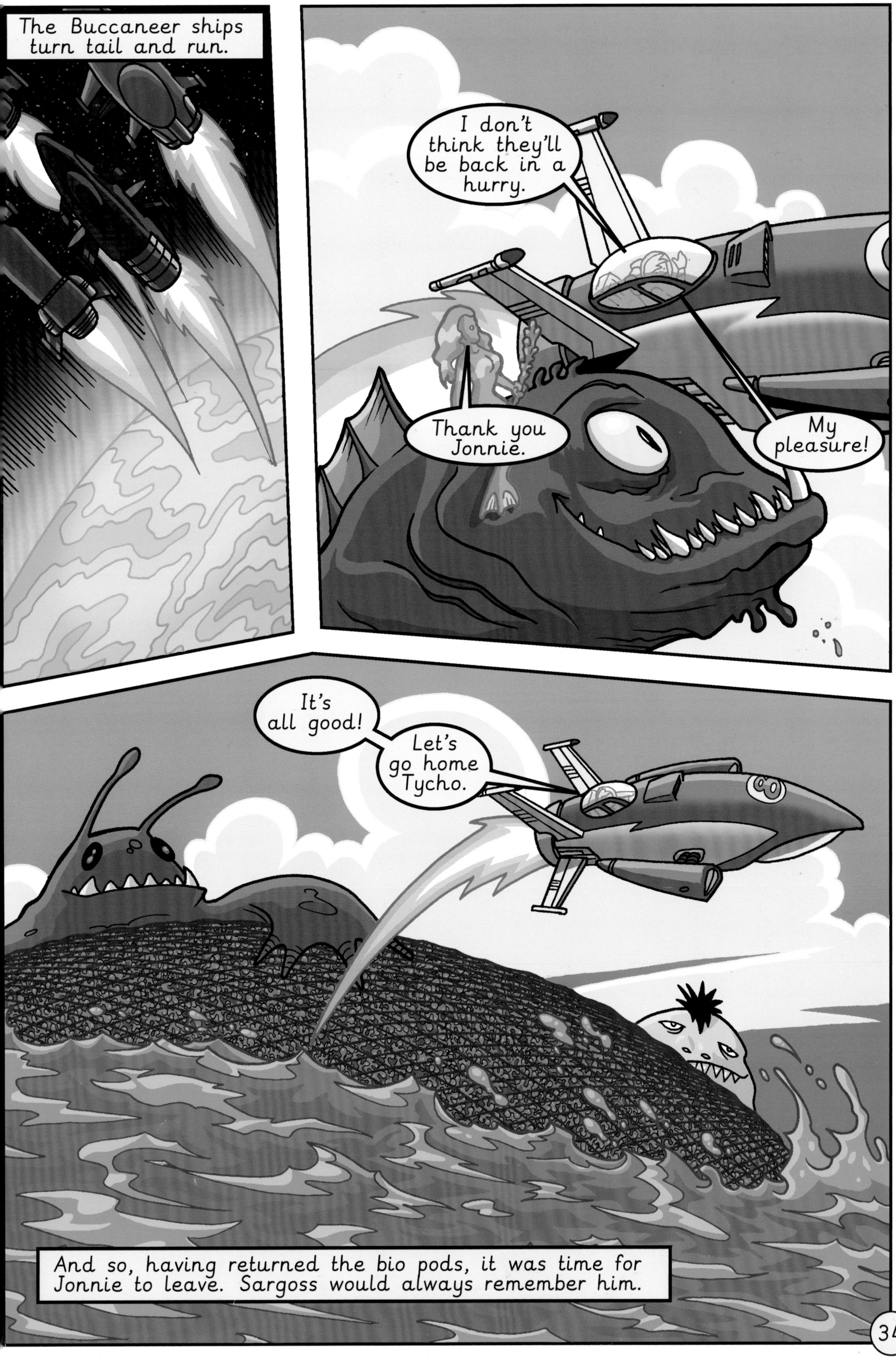
The Buccaneer ships turn tail and run.
I don't think they'll be back in a hurry.
Thank you Jonnie.
My pleasure!
It's all good!
Let's go home Tycho.
And so, having returned the bio pods, it was time for Jonnie to leave. Sargoss would always remember him.

The Sargasso Sea on Planet Earth:

•The Sargasso Sea is the name of a sea within the North Atlantic Ocean.

•It covers a huge area, 700 miles wide and 2000 miles long.

•It is the strangest sea on Planet Earth because it is the only 'sea' without a shoreline.

•Portugese sailors were one of the first people to discover the sea, way back in the 15th century, and they named it Sargasso after the Sargassum seaweed which grows there.

•The Sargassum seaweed can grow several metres long. It is usually brown or dark green and its fronds are covered in gas filled bladders, which help to keep the seaweed afloat. It has a rough sticky texture, but is very strong and flexible, which helps it to withstand the strong tidal currents of the North Atlantic.

•The Sargasso Sea has a notorious reputation! Historically, it was thought to be a threat to all who sailed there, as many ships became trapped and marooned. We now know that the ships were not trapped by the seaweed, but were simply becalmed there by the lack of winds.

•The water in the Sargasso Sea is really unusual; it is a wonderful deep blue colour and it is extremely clear. The underwater visibility in the sea is an amazing 60 metres!

•The Sargasso Sea plays a really important role in the migration of both the European and American eels. The eel larvae hatch there and swim all the way to Europe or to the east coast of North America. When they are mature, they then return to the Sargasso Sea to lay their own eggs there.

•Owing to the surface currents around the Sargasso Sea it unfortunately accumulates a huge amount of plastic waste products there. This is damaging our beautiful planet, which is why it's really important to always remember to re-cycle our plastic waste products carefully!

About the Author
John Chapman – Creator, Author

As a young boy, the wonder of the universe and a love of cycling had always been close to John's heart. Growing up in the 1960s John had begun to form the first concepts of an idea through his strong imagination and creative role-playing. He dreamt of rocket-ships and space adventures, and was passionate about his bicycle and the escapism it gave him. Therefore it was no surprise that in 1998 John had the idea for his imaginary character Jonnie Rocket.

With the creation of this character firmly embedded in John's imagination he spent the next two years formulating the idea; compiling the draft of his first book 'The Adventures of Jonnie Rocket' in the year 2000. He wrote this initial book as a scripted storyboard, with the aim of animating the character of Jonnie Rocket as a TV series.

John has since created a collection of stories, centred on 'The Adventures of Jonnie Rocket', twelve of which will be published in book form.

As part of John's imaginary space adventure, it was with some irony that in 1976 he found himself making a brief appearance as an X-Wing pilot in 'Star Wars (A New Hope)', living out the dream of a space adventurer through the most iconic sci-fi film of all time! Bringing Jonnie Rocket to life after four decades must surely be John Chapman's intention....

The Adventures of Jonnie Rocket: Books in the Series

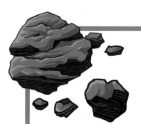

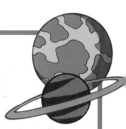

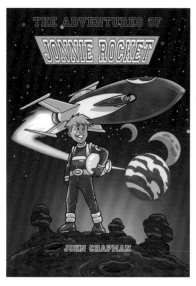

THE ADVENTURES OF
JONNIE ROCKET
JOHN CHAPMAN

THE ADVENTURES OF JONNIE ROCKET

ISBN: 978-0-9573035-0-8

Jonnie, aged 8, battles with Space Pirates and visits Zuke, a very strange planet.

THE ADVENTURES OF
JONNIE ROCKET
SAGA. 1
JOHN CHAPMAN

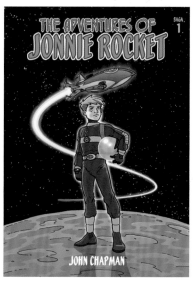

SAGA 1: THE RIDE OF TERROR

ISBN: 978-0-9573035-2-2

Jonnie, now aged 12, is on a mission to save the school bus. Will he succeed, or have the bullies gone too far this time?

THE ADVENTURES OF
JONNIE ROCKET
SAGA. 2
JOHN CHAPMAN

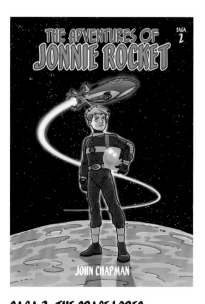

SAGA 2: THE SPACE LOBES

ISBN: 978-0-9573035-1-5

Jonnie crashes on Planet Cranium and meets the alien Space Lobes.

THE ADVENTURES OF
JONNIE ROCKET
SAGA. 3
JOHN CHAPMAN

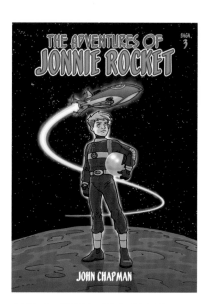

SAGA 3: THE SEA OF SARGOSS

ISBN: 978-0-9573035-3-9

Dr Avatar sends Jonnie to Sargoss, which is facing an ecological disaster of devastating proportions. Can he save the universe?

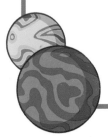

Become a Rocketeer: visit www.jonnierocket.com and learn more about Jonnie's world!